Ten Minutes on a June Morning

Ten Minutes on a June Morning

and other stories

by

FRANCIS CLIFFORD

HODDER AND STOUGHTON
LONDON SYDNEY AUCKLAND TORONTO

Contents

Acknowledgment

"The Watch" and "Ten Minutes on a June Morning" were originally published in *Argosy*; "The Walk Home" and "Summer Storm" were originally published in *Courier*; "Illusion and Reality" was originally published in the *London Evening News* as "The Waiter Who Sold Dreams"; "A Bear Called Priscilla" and "Green" (under the title "Christmas Gifts for a Green Man") were originally published in the *London Evening Standard*; "What Goes Up Must Come Down" was first published in *The Outspan*; "Turn and Turn About" was first published by Macmillan in *Winter's Crimes*, Vol IV.

Silence

When the wind dies,
and the hawk
searches in vain
for the rising air,
and there is no sound,
no sound at all
even on the edge of earshot;
then I can feel my scalp
tighten
and alarm is drawn across my soul.

Francis Clifford

Foreword

FRANCIS CLIFFORD WAS a remarkable writer. For the large majority of novelists the urge to convert some part of their mental processes into words on paper intended to arouse feelings in the minds of others is something acquired in very early days. Somehow or other—a sympathetic teacher, the example of a parent, a passion for reading—the match is put to the fire. But the boy who had been born Arthur Bell Thompson in Clifton, Bristol, in 1917, did not really begin writing until he was fully into man's estate and he started then because he saw the fiction form as the only way of unravelling a turmoil of discoveries he had had forced upon him by bitter experiences.

"That's what fiction is about, isn't it; finding out," he wrote to me once in a thank-you letter when he had seen in a review of his novel *Amigo, Amigo* that he had aroused in me the feelings he had had in his own mind (but I should have been thanking him).

For Francis Clifford writing was, right up until his death in 1975, this process of finding out. What at first he had to discover was the meaning of the revelations about people he had experienced during the horrors of the military campaign in Burma between 1941 and 1943. He was a member at the end of this period of Force 136 whose objects were, in the words

9

of the Official War History, "subversion, preparation of resistance movements and sabotage", and when his unit was at last forced to pull out he was left behind with a handful of others to blow bridges and survived a 1,000-mile jungle journey, much of the time surrounded by an unrelenting enemy, which left him a six-and-a-half stone skeleton with illnesses from which he never wholly recovered, as well as with recognition in the form of the D.S.O. "A lot of my friends," he told an interviewer thirty years later, "were badly tortured and had their heads cut off. And I think it was this knowledge of the way you might die and the pain and the suffering involved which changed the pattern of my looking at life." One of the stories in this volume gives us in a single chilled moment something of what such experiences must have meant directly.

Writing seemed to him after this the only way in which he could fasten down the discoveries he had made. And it did not come easily to him. He had never been at all an academic boy. At Christ's Hospital, the boarding school—where, incidentally, Coleridge, Lamb and the poet and essayist Leigh Hunt were educated—to which he went after he had been orphaned at the age of eight, he did well only on the playing field. And even when he had become a fully established novelist he said of himself, with typical understatement, "I use a very large rubber and a very small pencil."

After the war then, he set himself to sort things out by writing them down in the form of fiction. And it is characteristic of his quietness and modesty that he should have begun by writing simple short stories. Some of these, his earliest publications, are included in this volume. He chose to send them to editors using the name Francis Clifford, the surname composed of the first syllable of his own place of birth and the last syllable of Waterford in Ireland, the birthplace of his second wife to whose encouragement he continued to pay tribute all his writing life. These early pieces often show the limitations of their origins. A writer's being is not fulfilled until he has put on paper something that has been read by minds unknown to him. But short stories will see the light of day only if they comply with editors' stringent demands as to exact length and frequently as to a particular stereotype as well. Yet all of these pieces, even such a one as *Illusion and Reality* which comes complete with punch-line and fashionable cosmopolitan setting, are marked out by integrity of style, sign of the fundamental reason for which they were written.

Francis Clifford did not allow himself to try to make effects which were not there. His prose, even in the slightest of his tales like *The Walk Home* or the humorous *A Bear Called Priscilla* (which also shows the light-hearted side of sombre Army experience) is a careful series of steps, feeling its way across treacherous swamp and not advancing a yard further until what is behind is surely established. In much the same way the earlier stories explore, not the traumatic experiences of jungle warfare, but what was to be got, with hindsight, from the easier times he had experienced in the last days of the British Raj in Burma. To some of these stories—*Green*, *A Matter of Opinion*—one might apply the adjective Kiplingesque, though Francis Clifford shows little of the knowingness which was at one and the same time the virtue and the vice of the Kipling of India. But a story like *Cost Price* is full of that "it happened" feeling, another hallmark of Kipling's early work.

In all of the first stories, besides the honesty of the prose, one other thing is noticeable. The people in them are real, as real as their author can make them. He does not cheat characters to make a neat anecdote. Later in his most successful novels this will be one of the chief factors distinguishing him from the host of run-of-the-mill suspense writers: that however deep you plunge into his people you hit nowhere against the clanging metal of mere mechanical construction.

I have set the novels beside those of the host of simple suspense merchants, and it is right that they should be so placed. They set out like them to entertain their readers, to seize and to grip. Francis Clifford knew that there is little point in having something to say if you do not take whatever trouble is necessary to keep your hearers there while you say it. It was a lesson learnt in the hard commercial ways of short-story writing. And he found that what above all keeps an audience fast in its chairs is suspense. But suspense, he found too, has another, yet more valuable function. It exposes the people written about to a test. It is for them the equivalent of what the jungle had been for Arthur Thompson and his fellow fighters. And in that cruel, enemy-infested terrain the young soldier learnt a harsh and ever memorable lesson. "The war taught me that people are not what they seem," he said once. "The people I had thought were jolly good fellows and those whom I thought were absconders and slackers so often turned out to be the other way round." In the stories of his prime, *Twenty-minute Break*, *Turn and Turn About*, *Ten Minutes on a June Morning*, as in the novels, a man or a woman is exposed to a test to destruction-point and their creator finds out what happens to them.

It is because Francis Clifford's suspense situations are situations in which real people, characters as wholly imagined as the human beings who walk the world, are caught up that the books and the best of the stories are so much above the common run. With those other suspense merchants, even the most ingenious, you say "Yes, this is what it might be like if it happened to him". With Francis Clifford you say "This is what it would be like if it happened to me". He can take even the most banal situations, filmic situations the like of which we have seen a score of times on television—*A Bull for the Redhead* is an example from this collection—and yet by the searching flood of tender inquiry he brings to the people experiencing them, he makes us put ourselves in their place.

It is a tough method, tough on the imagined people who are put to the test, tough on the imaginer of their reactions, tough on the sensibilities of the reader who undergoes in his turn the ordeal. But there is no point in a test if it does not risk the component under strain breaking, and untested the component can never wholly be trusted. It is for this reason, because people with much good seen to be in them may eventually be shown as not being good enough, that there seems often to be an overwhelming pessimism in the Francis Clifford novels and in many of the stories, from the earliest *The Watch* on to the two long tales that complete the tally. But Clifford's pessimism was not a settled attitude in the light of which every human action is seen, as is that unique brand of pessimism which distinguishes a writer who has much in common with Clifford, Graham Greene. Clifford's pessimism is an ad hoc attitude. He puts a person to a hard test, that person does not on this occasion come out on top, Clifford records the fact. But there are occasions when, as in the Burma jungles, a pretty unlikely person does come out on top in a cruel test. And Clifford records the triumph, as in this collection with the convict in *Twenty-minute Break*.

There is, too, another aspect of Clifford's outlook that can result in us being given a picture of life that seems blackly depressing. It stems from his conviction, only a degree less part of his nature than his feeling that men under test show their true stature that people in our world are too often cynically manipulated. This too was something Arthur Thompson learnt in the harsh school of war. But he did not learn it in the jungle so much as afterwards when he was brought back to Britain shattered in health, and given a desk job in the Special Operations Executive London headquarters in Baker Street. Here too he made discoveries. "People that I was aware of were used," he told an interviewer many years later. "This is a circumstance which is, I suppose, permissible in war because one had to be ruthless in order to win. But these systems and the consequent blackmailing of people by authority still go on. And it's this that I find monstrous." He brought that sense of monstrous wrong both to his prize-winning story *Ten Minutes on a June Morning* and to the novels. It shows a sad side of human activity, but it is a side that exists and Clifford was right, knowing what he did, to hold it up for us to see.

Nor is his doing so wholly pessimistic. Like any good writer who incorporates into a work of fiction elements, whether of violence or sex or anything else, that are unpleasant to read

13

about in isolation, he by the mere act of writing episodes of violence in the context of a novel or a long short story put them in their place in the whole scheme of things. One of the reasons Francis Clifford was altogether able to do this, I think, was that shortly after his first failed marriage he found a religious faith and was received into the Roman Catholic Church. A little of that faith, which sustained him for the rest of a life beset by ill-health and until the success of *The Naked Runner* by some poverty, peeps out in a few of his stories, perhaps in the early ones a little awkwardly like a coat which is still new and has yet to settle comfortably on the shoulders. But this possession of a framework into which all of life could be placed certainly helped him to fit into his fictions those aspects of our earthly existence which can seem intolerably brutal. It is in the novels and stories where religion does not appear that it is most effective.

Perhaps it was Arthur Thompson's faith that gave him the chief characteristic that seems to me to shine in his work. It is modesty. He showed it too in the everyday transactions of life. But it was a modesty that had nothing in it of affected diffidence. It was a modesty that sprang from much inner certainty. I see it perhaps even more in the stories than in the novels. There is a temptation in writing a story, when there seems to be so little time in which to say anything, to exaggerate, to plunge on obtaining success by some dazzling coup. Francis Clifford does not succumb to this. Where he succeeds it is by saying no more than the story will bear. Very early he learnt, too, that true excitement is not generated by having an immense amount happen. It is generated by creating characters who are as near reality as the limitations of space will allow and who then, with the sympathy that this cannot but arouse, send tension springing up by undergoing even the simplest and slightest of ordeals.

Similarly, Clifford learnt, or knew instinctively, that it is a mistake to go further into people than is necessary for the purpose of what is being written about them at the time. He was exploring a character, not presenting one dished up and dissected on a plate. Not for him the cocky interior familiarities of so many magazine-story writers. And, as I have already said, his prose, the sort of words he used and the sort of way he put them together, breathes this very spirit of careful exploration into delicate territory, the inside of real human beings. One can sense often the number of times that that large rubber must have obliterated something the small pencil had written which was not quite exact.

So that in the end the words which were allowed to appear in print, though they are simple and altogether unshowy, ring with authority. He may describe a scene that has nothing particularly exciting or gripping about it—almost all the stories in this volume begin in this way—and yet one's attention is held. The sheer exactitude does it. He has seen what he describes—although it may never have happened at all in this world—and he picks out just the details that will lob that vision, like a hand-grenade, to explode in the distant reader's mind. This did happen, you feel. You have it on authority.

The ability to conjure up scenes that an unknown reader will see and will remember is the quality that Francis Clifford shares with a select handful of English writers down the ages. Many novelists cannot achieve the vividness—notice how in *Turn and Turn About* the moment of the boat landing on dangerous territory is suddenly made sharply real by just the few words "they could smell the weed growths"—and of those who can achieve this vividness many lack the force of authority behind their descriptions, whether of places or of people, the force that gives the second quality, memorability. Of course, not every story here has this, though all I think show the promise of what was to come and are worth having for that alone.

Francis Clifford made you see and he made you remember. How sad that they are the last gleanings of a very considerable talent.

H. R. F. KEATING

15

The Watch

FROM THE AGE of ten Ba Chit had set his heart on serving the Colonel, rejecting with youthful disdain his parents' suggestion that he should eventually find a job in a rice mill or join forces with his cousin on one of the stalls in the open-air market. Either of these occupations, the boy argued, might be good enough for the friends with whom he played ball on the patch of wasteland near his home and shared the dust thrown up by the Colonel's car as it raced through the sun-gutted streets, but neither would be good enough for him. His mind was made up. Nor would pedalling a tri-shaw suit him, or trying his hand as an under-gardener at the Zoological Gardens where his father worked and was more than ready to put in a word on his behalf. For Colonel Rance, who lived in one of the largest houses in Rangoon and ran a flourishing import-export agency from an important-looking office in the city's business quarter, was Ba Chit's idol, and nothing would satisfy him but that, when he was old enough, he should be allowed to wait on the Colonel hand and foot.

Now and again a heartfelt wish materialises for us all. And in the fullness of time, when Ba Chit was just fourteen, he achieved his first great ambition. He was taken on as second house-boy to the Colonel, and the devoted enthusiasm with which he applied himself to his many duties made his employer more than satisfied with his choice. On several occasions Colonel Rance warmly complimented the boy on the thoroughness of his work, and when that happened Ba Chit was beside himself with pride. Never in his short life had he been so happy and, although the Colonel quarrelled incessantly with his wife, nothing occurred during his first few months in the house to change his belief that the Colonel was indeed a king amongst men.

Ba Chit's second ambition was to own the sort of wrist-watch Colonel Rance possessed. It was unique in his experience, quite unlike any watch he had ever seen anywhere. Not only did it tell the time, but the day of the week, the day of the month and the month itself; in addition it also indicated the phases of the moon. When he went into the bedroom in the mornings Ba Chit would see it on the bedside table, and sometimes, if the Colonel was still asleep, he would pick it up and study it more closely, marvelling that so small a piece of mechanism could provide so much information. Truly it was a magnificent watch, and it seemed only natural that a man of Colonel Rance's importance should possess such an incomparable treasure.

The boy knew it was the custom for a servant to receive an occasional gift, and early on he decided that if ever he was given the opportunity of stating a preference in this respect a watch of identical ingenuity would be his unhesitating choice. The Colonel was not an ungenerous employer—the senior house-boy had been presented with a portable transistor radio, made as far away as Hong Kong, as a New Year gift—and although Ba Chit had his feet sufficiently on the ground to know that he could hardly expect a watch cased in gold, he was more than ready to settle for base metal.

Ba Chit was too young and his English too sketchy, to understand what Colonel Rance and his wife so often quarrelled about. But he could not help noticing that his employer usually seemed to be defending himself. The Colonel was never the one to start the arguments and most of the time he appeared to make repeated denials. When the trouble was

18

over—and occasionally before—as often as not he would drive away in the car and only return to the house at a very late hour. From time to time Ba Chit would be roused from his own bed in order to undress the Colonel and help to get him into his, and at moments like these he found himself possessed of an intense dislike of Mrs. Rance for having caused his hero to reduce himself to such a mumbling, reeking, undignified condition.

The senior house-boy, with long and varied experience of Europeans, insisted that the Colonel was fifty-six and Mrs. Rance forty-seven. But Ba Chit remained privately of the opinion that, if anything, it was the other way round. Colonel Rance's deep-tanned features were almost unlined, and though his hair was grey he looked by far the younger of the two. Mrs. Rance, who had extremely pale eyes and a dry leathery complexion, could no more have been forty-seven than Mandalay was still the capital of Burma. Or so he told himself. What was more, when at his best the Colonel seemed a particularly youthful person, much given to laughter and breaking into snatches of song, as well as keeping himself fit on the golf course, the tennis courts and in the exercise room at the back of the house where there was a cycling machine and a collection of old leather-covered dumb-bells. Whereas Mrs. Rance, who rarely laughed, never sang and seemed to have no relaxation other than a thrice-weekly bridge session, was thin, tight-lipped and surely too sour in spirit for her purported years.

But everyone is occasionally guilty of misjudging another. One day, in his sixth month in the Colonel's household, Mrs. Rance sent for Ba Chit and informed him that she was going away for a week. His face betrayed no emotion: "Very good" was all he said, and waited to be dismissed. However, Mrs. Rance had not finished; in addition she was actually smiling at him, which was something he could not remember having happened until then. Mrs. Rance pointed out in her limited, hand-waving version of Burmese that because she knew how devoted he was to her husband she was particularly anxious

19

that he should take especially good care of him during her enforced absence.

Ba Chit was delighted to be so honoured. His dislike of her softened immediately and he eagerly agreed to her suggestion that he should move his bed-roll into the house whilst she was away and guard the Colonel both day and night. Vaguely, Mrs. Rance referred to the danger of dacoits, thieves and other good-for-nothings who might imperil her husband's safety and their joint possessions. It never occurred to Ba Chit to question why such a precaution should be necessary when locks and bars were normally considered sufficient. Mrs. Rance was all sweetness and light, and to the boy there seemed absolutely no significance in the fact that she gave him ten rupees when he promised her, with shining eyes, to position himself outside the Colonel's bedroom door each night and to confine himself to the house during the day. And although the Colonel himself was far from enthusiastic when told of the arrangement later that evening, he reluctantly agreed to Ba Chit doing as Mrs. Rance wished.

The rains come to Burma in May and the preceding few weeks are unbearably hot. In the corridor leading off the Colonel's bedroom the atmosphere was stifling. On the first night Ba Chit slept only a little, on the second not at all. There was neither fan nor window in the enclosed space where he lay. By the third night he was so tired that he could hardly keep his eyes open, yet sleep was still impossible and he felt he would suffocate unless he got some air. Repeatedly he told himself that he had promised to guard the Colonel and endeavoured to find encouragement by reflecting on the honour which had befallen him rather than to any other of the servants. But to no avail. At last he succumbed and moved his bed-roll on to a nearby verandah, where he stretched out under the moon and the vast stars and was unconscious almost as soon as his head went down.

Guilt troubled Ba Chit with the comparative coolness of a blood-red dawn. He at once retreated to the corridor so that Colonel Rance should believe that he had not been deserted.

He did the self-same thing on succeeding nights, and it seemed unlikely that he was suspected of failing in his duty because the Colonel went out of his way to be more than usually affable to him as the week ran to its close.

There was no break-in. Nothing was stolen from the house and the Colonel's person was not threatened. All should have been well. But on the day that Mrs. Rance returned from wherever she had been there was the fiercest quarrel of any until then between the two of them. She came hurrying out of the bedroom with an article of clothing which Ba Chit did not recognise and waved it in front of her husband, apparently demanding an explanation. Colonel Rance went a dull sort of red under his mahogany tan and began to shout his answers, which Ba Chit knew from past experience to be a bad sign. In contrast Mrs. Rance was very pale in her anger, but kept stamping her right foot.

Ba Chit, who had followed her when she emerged from the bedroom, decided that there were more sensible places to be and began discreetly to withdraw. But Mrs. Rance suddenly seemed to notice him for the first time; wheeling on him she wanted to know whether anyone except her husband and the servants had entered the bedroom while she was away.

Impassively, Ba Chit shook his head. It was embarrassing to be confronted in such a fashion in the Colonel's presence, and in any case he did not understand the reason for Mrs. Rance's fury.

"Are you speaking the truth?"

Ba Chit nodded.

Mrs. Rance stared at him accusingly, something small and soft and pink crumpled in her fingers. There was a long pause. Then she asked: "How well did you keep your promise to me?"

For seconds on end Ba Chit hesitated. It was impossible to avoid giving a direct answer. He had cheated and must admit it. But as he opened his mouth to speak he caught sight of the Colonel's face and, in a flash, he realised that he would never be able to bring himself to say that he had wilfully failed him.

So he lied, earnestly and with desperate conviction, and swore to Mrs. Rance that he had done exactly as she had required.

It was not until much later, by which time he had come to know something of the sad ways of the world, that Ba Chit understood why the very next morning Colonel Rance presented him with the wrist-watch he had admired for so long, and why it was that when the Colonel handed it to him he did so with a heavy wink and said nothing at all.

Ba Chit sold the watch, of course. It never again had the same pure magical fascination for him. After the inevitable bargaining he got five hundred rupees for it and, much to his parents' satisfaction, established himself in the open-air market on a stall alongside that of his cousin. Disillusion is a part of growing up, though there is consolation in all things. But no one—least of all a boy—likes to be fooled, especially in such a way and by someone who meant so much.

The Walk Home

A GREAT BRUISED fist of cloud was slowly pressing the sun into the distant claret-coloured hills as the two of them made their way across the paddy-fields. In half an hour darkness would be on them, and they walked quickly despite their fatigue, the Burmese boy, lagging a little , carrying the gun over his shoulder. There was still nearly a mile to go before they reached the track leading to the road, and even then it was quite a distance to where they had parked the car a few hours earlier.

It had not been a successful afternoon's shooting. Two brace of snipe were all they had to show for their pains and, although he would never have admitted it, the boy was conscious of a deep sense of disappointment. For months he had been longing for the opportunity of accompanying his master on such a trip; but now, aching in every muscle and with scratched legs smarting angrily, he was only aware of feeling that his part in the day's proceedings had been far from satisfactory. The small number of birds had something to do with it, of course, though perhaps, even if there had been others, all the discomfort might still have seemed no more worthwhile. What really troubled him, as the afternoon wore on and they tramped and scrambled across the wide, seemingly endless sweep of paddy and marshland, was a steadily mounting suspicion that almost anyone else in his position would have done better.

23

Back in the bungalow it was a very different matter. Though he was young—and therefore inclined to attach too much importance to himself—he knew that his many duties about the house made him almost indispensable and, because he loved his master, he carried them out with enthusiastic efficiency. But today, from the moment they left the car, he felt completely out of his element. The difficulty was that he did not fully understand what was expected of him. When the first birds came over he had been caught unprepared, gaping excitedly upwards, heedless of the other's shout for more cartridges. By the time they were ready it was too late, but in the flurry of fumbling for them he failed to mark the spot where a bird had fallen and spent a good ten minutes searching for it afterwards. And so it had gone on, with variations, over and over again throughout the long afternoon. There was never a word of complaint, but he doubted if he would be asked to come again. When they eventually turned for home and it was too late to make amends, weariness and dejection claimed him and even being given the gun to carry was insufficient to cheer his jaded spirits.

They moved along the narrow, low ridges between the paddy-fields, the man limping slightly; neither saying a word. Somewhere far behind them a jackal howled suddenly, and a flock of white egrets beat silently overhead on their way towards the river. The light still held, but already the sun was half-way down behind the hills and, here and there, long fingers of mist were stretching out across the plain.

It was the boy who first saw the snake. They were skirting a shallow, overgrown gully when, chancing to look up, he caught sight of the thing moving in their direction. It came fast, as fast as a hare at full stretch, neck arched, swan-like, eighteen inches above the ground; hood flattened and extended below its head. Even in the first moment of panic he noticed all that quite clearly.

"Snake! Snake!" he screamed, eyes dilated and stomach

turning to water. "Snake, *thakin*! . . . Run! . . . Run quickly!"

The man saw it almost at once. For a fraction of a second he seemed unable to move—then, slewing suddenly on his heels, he started to run, stumbling desperately over the marshy ground.

Despite his terror the boy had thought only of his master. Now, standing there helplessly, with all the strength gone out of his legs, he saw the snake veer off its line of attack and swing in towards him. The thing was only about twenty yards away when he remembered the gun. As he dragged it frantically off his left shoulder and brought it across into a firing position he could hear the noise of the cobra coming through the short paddy like a gust of wind.

It was nearly on him when he fired. The recoil sent the butt smashing against his collar-bone, yet, even as he staggered backwards, his finger snatched at the second trigger and once again he felt the gun jump in his hands. Then he dropped it and began running, running blindly, with his head down and his breath coming in great sobs of fear; running like a madman . . . anywhere . . . anywhere to get away.

He had gone perhaps fifty yards when he heard his master shouting. For a moment or two he paid no attention and continued to plunge forward until, hearing his voice again, he risked a glance over his shoulder. Nothing was following him: the grass and paddy immediately behind were undisturbed except by his own headlong flight. He slowed down and clambered on to the largest of a group of ant-heaps topping one of the ridges between the fields so as to get a better view. There was no sign of the snake; no sign of anything except the man waving to him in the half-light and calling to him to come back. He retraced his steps slowly, with the sweat going cold on him and a desire to vomit taking hold as his nerves began to relax.

What was left of the snake lay, still twitching, within five yards of the gun. The man, the colour gone from his face, smiled at the boy as he came up. The shock was over.

"You had a close shave," he said. "Are you all right?"

"Yes, *thakin*." He looked at the headless thing on the ground and shuddered. "It is a very big one."

"What sort is it?"

"Hamadryad, *thakin* . . . King cobra."

His master nodded. "I thought it must be." He touched it with his foot. "Reckon it was nearly eight feet long when it was all there."

The boy did not say anything. He was still feeling sick, but his eyes lit up when the other spoke again. "Didn't know you could handle a gun. Next time we come out, you must try your hand at something a bit more pleasant."

They had found the track now and it was only a matter of minutes before they reached the car. The boy no longer lagged behind his master. He was up alongside, stretching his short, torn legs so as to keep in step, the gun at a jaunty angle over his shoulder. His fatigue and nausea had vanished and he carried himself with pride as the two of them moved through the swiftly gathering dusk.

It had been a wonderful day. On the long walk home he had shown himself to be a man.

At the Foot of the Hill

THE TWO NATIVES, their knees bent under the weight of the huge black pig slung between them on a sagging bamboo pole, shouted to Father O'Connor as they emerged from the jungle into the clearing.

The priest jumped excitedly to his feet. "Just look at that beauty!" he exclaimed with enthusiasm. Hurrying to the top of the flight of rickety steps that led down from the verandah he called out something Roberts didn't understand, and the taller of the two half-naked men grunted a staccato reply. The priest waved a hand in acknowledgment and retorted with a few words which made the sweating carriers grin from ear to ear.

Roberts walked across to join him, and together they watched the pig being carried along the path towards the village.

"That means fresh pork for dinner," the priest smiled delightedly. "A great improvement, I might say, on what I would otherwise have been forced to offer you."

"It's a hell of a size," Roberts said bluntly.

"Big or small, it'll be most welcome. I haven't tasted pork for the best part of three months."

For the first time since he arrived unheralded at the mission house an hour or so earlier the prospector realised that his presence there might be an embarrassment. He was willing to

27

pay, of course, but he could see that, in this grim wilderness of hill and jungle, money was of little consequence.

"Are you sure I'm not an unwelcome guest?" he asked suddenly.

"Unwelcome?" Father O'Connor laughed. "My dear fellow—"

"I had no idea things were so tough up here. If you know of another place I'd willingly move on."

"Nonsense! I'm delighted to be your host. It's not often that I have company and, thanks to our friend the pig, food is no longer a serious problem." He laid his hand on Roberts' arm. "Besides, if you want to explore that range of hills, this is by far the best base to work from. There isn't another person within fifty miles who could put you up."

"It's . . . it's very good of you," Roberts said lamely. He looked after the disappearing hillmen and nodded in their direction. "What do those men hunt with? They're only carrying knives."

The priest made his way back to his chair. "It's not really a case of hunting—not active hunting, that is. They set traps in likely places and inspect them every day. A weapon isn't necessary. Whatever they find in the trap is usually dead by the time they get to it."

"Why is that?" the prospector asked. "Poison?"

"No. No—they don't use poison. They dig a pit, fill it with sharpened bamboo stakes and cover the hole over. Each of those stakes is like a rapier." Father O'Connor made a gesture with his hands. "There's no active hunting. I suppose it would be more correct to say that the animal gives itself up." He smiled again. "The only trouble is that it doesn't happen often enough. Fresh meat is something of a luxury in this part of the world."

Roberts sat down at the other side of the table, and stared curiously at the tired, drawn face of the priest. He wanted to ask more about the trapping, but instead he reverted to what he had been about to say when the men with the pig interrupted the conversation.

28

"With a name like O'Connor I suppose you must be Irish, but I'd never have placed you by your accent."

"No?"

"No. Had me fooled there. What part are you from?"

"Just outside Portadown. I don't expect you've heard of the village. It's a very small place." The priest screwed up his eyes, trying to visualise it, but the impression he got was vague and indistinct. It all seemed a long way off; a long time ago.

Roberts thought for a moment. "Portadown. That's *Northern* Ireland, isn't it?"

"That's right."

"But I thought you were a Roman Catholic."

Father O'Connor chuckled. "So I am. I don't have to come from the Free State to be a Catholic. One's faith has nothing to do with national boundaries. If it had, I shouldn't be here."

"I guess not," the prospector said after a pause. "To be honest with you religion isn't a subject I know much about. Hardly given it a thought since I was a kid." He scratched the back of his head and, encouraged by the other's silence, went on. "Reckon I shouldn't be telling you this, but if you were to ask me to say the Lord's Prayer I wouldn't be able to get all the way through it."

"I could soon teach it you," the priest said.

"I'm sure," Roberts said awkwardly. He realised that he was on dangerous ground, and cursed himself for his stupidity in talking so unwisely. These priests are all the same, he thought irritably. It was a long while since he had been in contact with any of them, and, now that he was living under the same roof as one, he could see that he would have to be more careful about what he said.

"How long have you been out here?" he asked, quickly changing the subject.

"Six years."

"In this place?"

"Yes."

Roberts whistled. "What about home leave?"

"I don't have it," Father O'Connor said quietly. "This *is* my

29

home. Maybe I'll be moved to another area, but I'll never return to Ireland."

Roberts stared out over the great rolling sea of evergreen jungle stretching away from the foot of the hill and asked himself what manner of man it was who could voluntarily spend his life in such surroundings. He'd found himself in some out-of-the-way places in his time and knew something of solitude, but never for long. Never for more than a few months at the outside. And there had always been a reason—gold, perhaps, or tin, or wolfram—but, whatever it was, there had always been a reason, and, as often as not, something to show for it afterwards.

But what about this priest? What did he hope to achieve in a place like this? Teach a few prayers to the natives; try to change whatever beliefs they held . . . and what then? It was something he could not understand. He prided himself on being a practical man and it seemed nothing less than a stupid waste, even allowing for the possibility of a general conversion. People should be left alone to decide such matters for themselves. There were plenty of other things, worthwhile things, to be done.

He transferred his gaze to the priest, noticing the sunken, feverish eyes and the nervous movement of the pale hands. "Those men carrying the pig . . . Are they Christians?"

Father O'Connor shook his head. "I'm afraid not. I haven't had a great many converts so far."

"How many?"

"Five."

At first Roberts imagined he had heard incorrectly. "I thought you said five," he grinned.

"So I did. This is a new area for the Church and, in the circumstances, I believe progress has been very good."

For a few minutes Roberts was too astonished to say anything further. Six years for five converts! No wonder his companion had offered to teach him the Lord's Prayer so promptly!

Later on, throughout the afternoon and during dinner,

their conversation touched on a variety of subjects, but he was always conscious of the wide gulf between him and the priest. It was a gulf that could only be bridged by sympathy and understanding, and he had neither to offer. To him the whole thing seemed a ridiculous, fantastic waste of time, made all the more preposterous by the pitiful lack of success attending it.

And yet, to his surprise, he was troubled by his inability to understand. When he went to bed he lay for quite an hour, watching the fireflies outside the mosquito-net, trying to discover what possible compensation even five hundred converts could be for an existence such as this. Then, eventually, he slept. He woke once during the night, as if to escape from a confused dream in which he stood with Father O'Connor on the verandah watching five natives being carried up the hill slung under bamboo poles, while the priest remarked: "There's no active hunting. I suppose it would be more correct to say that they gave themselves up. The trouble is that it doesn't happen often enough."

After that he did not wake again until morning.

The priest always said Mass at seven o'clock. He rose at daybreak, as usual, and it was not until he had almost finished dressing that he remembered he had a guest in the next room. He was so accustomed to being on his own . . .

What was the fellow's name? Roberts—yes, that was it. A freelance prospector, or something of the sort. He wasn't sure what the newcomer did exactly, and he hadn't been able to bring himself to ask too many questions. All he knew was that the man wanted to spend a few days examining the big ridge to the east, though what he hoped to find there Father O'Connor couldn't think.

He tiptoed cautiously along the verandah and glanced in through the open door at the big, red-faced man lying under the net. The prospector was still sleeping and, seeing him again through the veil of the netting, the priest recalled with sorrow that he was as much in need of conversion as were the

31

natives amongst whom he had worked for the past six years. Nationality had nothing to do with it. Only yesterday he had explained that, and the man to whom he had explained it provided the proof. For a moment the thought entered his mind that perhaps he could have served God equally well by devoting himself to bringing His message to his own countrymen. There must be many who were in need of it and the life would have been incomparably easier. A feeling of despair took hold of him as he turned and looked across the surface of the dark green jungle, aware, as never before, of the silence and loneliness of the years that were past—and were still to come.

He retraced his steps along the verandah. He was sickening for another bout of fever and it needed all his strength to throw off the sense of depression. By the time he had vested himself and entered the tiny, bare chapel the mood had passed. As he gave thanks to God for the opportunity of making Him known to those who inhabited the hills and valleys of this huge jungle country, the thought of his five converts filled his heart with joy, and he knew again that these were the people who needed him most.

Memento, Domine, famulorum, famularumque, tuarem . . .

Father O'Connor paused for a moment, then added the name of the sleeping man in the other room to his prayers.

Roberts opened the flap of the mosquito-net and swung his legs over the side of the bed. He could hear the voice of the priest through the thin walls of the mission house, and guessed that it came from the chapel. For a moment or two he sat, listening; then, shaking his head in dismissal of the same thoughts that had troubled him the previous day, he got up and started to shave.

The pair of them breakfasted on the verandah half an hour later. It was still cool and Roberts was anxious to get moving before the sun rose much higher in the empty sky. Once or twice during the meal he looked at the long bare ridge sticking out of the sea of jungle like a sandbank, and made a rough guess that it was about eight miles away. The priest thought it was more, a couple of miles further perhaps, for the track twisted around the hill contours a good deal. That was all the better reason for wanting to make an early start. If he set off immediately he ought, with luck, to reach the top of the ridge by mid-day. He would then have a few hours to give it a pre-liminary once-over before returning to base. But it would be tough going, with the sun burning him up most of the way.

The prospector left the table and collected what he required from his room. Father O'Connor came with him to the top of the steps and, for the second time that morning, offered to arrange for one of the natives from the village to accompany him.

"It's a fair track most of the way," the priest said. "But I'd feel happier if you had a guide. I'd come myself if it wasn't for this fever."

Roberts grinned cheerfully. "I prefer being on my own," he said. "Always have. But thanks just the same." He lifted the ruck-sack on to his shoulders and clattered down the steps. "Well—see you this evening. I'll tell you all about it."

"If you aren't back by sundown I'll assume you're stopping the night at one of the villages—though I wouldn't recom-mend it. Good luck!"

Father O'Connor stood at the end of the verandah and watched the heavy, red-faced man crossing the clearing. A spasm of nausea gripped him momentarily and he closed his eyes until it had passed. When he looked again towards the path leading to the village the prospector had gone.

It was nearly sundown now, and Roberts was worried. High overhead the last of the sunlight splintered on the matted roof of the jungle, but at ground level it was already dark enough for him to have difficulty in keeping to the track.

He looked at his watch, the luminous dial showing faintly in the green gloom. Just on six—more than a quarter of an hour since he last checked, which meant he must have covered at least a mile.

It couldn't be much further now, he reassured himself. Half a mile at the outside. Once he struck the foot of the hill and climbed out of the jungle he could hardly go wrong. From there it was less than ten minutes up to the village; another two or three hundred yards to the mission house. That would seem the longest stretch of all, of course. The last bit invariably did when you were all in.

He stumbled over the exposed roots of a tree and cursed loudly. God, he was tired! It had been a brute of a day and he'd made matters worse by staying too long on the ridge. He knew that now. Tomorrow he'd make an earlier start to ensure having plenty of time to look around and get back while the light held. He'd feel all right in the morning; a night's rest would see him in good shape again, though, at the moment, he felt he never wanted to walk another step.

A creeper brushed against his face, and he clawed it away with his hands. If only he could see properly! He peered anxiously into the gathering darkness and, urged on by a sudden tremor of panic, increased his pace. The track seemed to veer a little to the left and he followed it trustingly. It was not until he found himself pushing, breast-high, through some undergrowth that he realised he had gone the wrong way.

At that moment, through a break in the lacework of trees, he got a glimpse of the hill straight ahead, with the mission house, still catching the sunlight, perched like a square brown box on the summit. With an exclamation of relief he stumbled forward again. He took two paces and felt the ground collapse suddenly beneath him. His agonised scream as a forest of bamboo stakes impaled him rose from the pit and echoed through the cavernous vault of the dark jungle, setting the unseen monkeys chattering excitedly amongst the branches overhead.

He was lying diagonally across the pit; the heels of his boots just touching the ground and his arched body supported, at half-a-dozen points, by the pressure of wood on bone. His head, thrown back in the first blinding moment of agony, rested against a stone protruding from the side of the pit. Both arms were outstretched, flung wide as he tried to save himself when he fell, his right hand pinned through the centre of the palm.

Held thus, unable to move anything except his head and left arm, he alternated between consciousness and merciful oblivion. He knew nothing of the passing of the hours. Three times during the night his brain cleared and, as the severed nerves and torn muscles twitched and contracted viciously along the length of his body, his cries shattered the silence of the darkness. Throughout these conscious moments his left hand plucked feebly at the bamboo stakes. Now and then he lifted his head to listen, believing he heard voices. And all the while the blood collected in a spreading pool beneath him, and the weight of his body, made more heavy by the bulging ruck-sack across his shoulders, pressed him relentlessly down on to the slim, murderous lances of hardened wood.

He screamed, but his voice cracked and trailed away in a great choking sob, and he started to vomit.

Over the edge of the pit, through the ragged break in the trees, he could see the mission house at the top of the hill, a tiny square silhouette against the skyline. He stared at it desperately with glazed eyes and began to shout again.

Surely they could hear him? . . .

Time passed. He tried to move his legs, but there was no strength in them. They didn't seem to belong to him any more. He lifted his head. He could hear nothing; nothing except the blood dripping into the bottom of the pit, and, as a fresh wave of pain began to rush through him, he realised with terror that unless they found him quickly he would probably die. Until then it hadn't occurred to him. He had only been conscious of the tremendous, stabbing shock from over a score of wounds that tore simultaneously at every part of him in a series of shuddering crescendoes.

The thought of death was in his mind as he screamed again at the black blob of the mission house. Hurry, blast you! Hurry! Do something! Come quickly! . . . Quickly! . . .

His free hand beat a wild, frenzied tattoo on the bamboo

35

stakes around him and then, as the darkness closed in suddenly, he fainted.

When he opened his eyes a second time the moon was hanging over the hill-top like a big ripe orange. The pain had eased for the moment. He felt cold and leaden, and very tired.

Suddenly something moved in the undergrowth close by and he craned his head forward.

"Help! . . . Help!" he croaked.

No one answered. There was a swift scuttle in the shadows, followed by silence. He tried to focus his eyes on the mission house, but all he could make out was a distant, unsteady blur. Then he was sick again, and the searing agony began to throb through him anew . . .

His mind was racing. They were a long time coming, he thought. They'd have to hurry. He couldn't hold out much longer. The natives would find him in the morning; he knew that, because the priest had told him they inspected the traps each day. But he couldn't last until then. Death was very close now. He could feel it in his legs already. Sometimes it moved into his stomach, and it was then that he started to vomit. Yesterday he'd meant to ask the priest how long it took to die in one of these pits. Now he was going to find out. He started to laugh, a dry, broken laugh that turned slowly into a whimpering groan as the pain raked his body from end to end . . .

His eyes began to close, and a confused succession of memories passed through his fevered brain. They meant nothing to him now, nothing; and many of them he had hoped to forget.

He wasn't afraid of death any more. But he wanted the priest to come. The others didn't matter. He knew that he was going to die and there were a lot of things he wanted to ask the priest, if there was still time. A lot of things. Things he'd never bothered about before and, even until yesterday, had found it impossible to understand . . .

He tried to call out, but no sound came. His tongue was a thick, swollen slab, flapping stupidly in a cracked, leathery cell of a mouth.

36

Then he felt death come into his stomach, and once more the darkness flooded over him.

There was no moon now, but it was growing lighter. Dawn. The stricken man moved his head slightly and stared upwards into the high, cathedral-like roof of the jungle.

His lips moved as he prayed. He wished the priest had come so that he could have been taught what to say. It was too late to ask all the questions that were still unanswered, but, if nothing more, he would have liked to have been able to go right through to the end of the Lord's Prayer . . .

He looked towards the top of the hill. The sun was just touching the mission house. For a brief moment he saw the building more clearly than at any time before. Then his vision clouded over.

It was ending now. There was no more pain; but death was lying in his stomach all the time and, as he heard the gruff murmur of native voices in the still morning air, he gave himself up to it.

Two days later, towards evening, Father O'Connor sat in his room, weak from the fever, writing his monthly report. It was a longer report than usual, for it contained much of the information that had already been sent by runner to the police in the nearest town, to which he added some details of the burial service he had conducted that morning.

When he had finished he read the report through carefully. It was only then that he realised he had made no mention of the progress of his work since he had last written, and he inserted a final paragraph to the effect that the number of conversions in the area was still five.

He was not to know that it would have been more accurate if he had increased the number by one.

Green

THIS HAPPENED A good many years ago—before the war. I was just twenty-one at the time and had been in Burma for exactly three weeks. You could tell how long the others had been out there by the colour of their arms and knees. Hobbs, for instance—he was my immediate boss—sported a dark shade of mahogany. Mine were the lightest of light oak. And in every other respect I was about as green as could be.

I lived alone then in an isolated bungalow on the banks of a huge brown river which seemed to be permanently in flood. My work usually ended an hour or so before sundown and, after a shower and a change of clothes, I was in the habit of driving off somewhere for dinner. I'd dropped cards right, left and centre soon after my arrival and the residents of that particular backwater were evidently curious to discover what sort of new blood the ship had brought out from England, for there was no shortage of invitations.

That particular evening I'd scarcely finished dressing when my house-boy announced that someone wished to see me.

"Who is it?" I asked, in what was meant to be Burmese.

"A Sikh, *thakin*."

"A Sikh?" I essayed another mouthful of tonal vowels. "Ask him to come up, will you?"

The bungalow was built on piles and the stairs led up to a banistered hole in the floor of the lounge. I got there just as the Sikh emerged. He was a magnificent figure, a giant of a man well in excess of six feet and built in proportion. He greeted me with a formal flourish.

"Good evening, Mr. Clifford."

"Good evening." I couldn't imagine how he knew my name, but it was a relief to find that he spoke English. "What can I do for you?"

He smiled. "It is very kind of you to forgive this intrusion." It was good English, too; not the comic Welsh variety most of them used. "My reason for coming is to wish you a Merry Christmas."

"Christmas," I repeated, somewhat taken aback.

"Yes, Mr. Clifford. Your great Christian festival."

Christmas, it was true, was only three or four days away, but with frogs croaking a tropical chorus outside the windows and sweat needling my scalp and neck I found the fact almost impossible to believe. The calendar was as confusing as everything else just then.

Rather lamely I said, "That's very kind of you. Very kind of you indeed."

He bowed slightly. "I have taken the liberty of bringing you a small gift. I hope you will not find it unacceptable."

He clapped his hands, whereupon six coolies mounted dramatically into the room, each shouldering a wooden crate. They lined up facing me like a squad of recruits, lowered the crates to the floor, then loped silently away down the stairs.

"Scotch whisky," the Sikh said, pointing to the boxes in turn. "Gin. Crystallised fruits. Mixed fruit squashes. Christmas puddings. And mince tarts." He stood back, smiling enigmatically. "All straight from the cold store in Rangoon. As I have already said, I hope you will find them acceptable."

I was too astonished to thank him adequately. The whole business was so completely unexpected that I hadn't really grasped what was happening. I offered him a drink, but he refused. A cigarette, then, or a cheroot? It seemed the very least I could do. But he declined and, after again wishing me the compliments of the season, he withdrew, descending through the floor somewhat like a pantomime genie making an exit.

Baffled, I returned to the bedroom, telling myself that it was probably the custom for local merchants to do this sort of thing. Obviously, though, I would have to mention it to Hobbs, if only to find out where I stood if anything like it were ever to happen again.

I was still brushing my hair when my house-boy re-appeared. "There is a Sikh to see you, *thakin*."

"A Sikh?"

"*Another* Sikh, *thakin*," he said impassively.

I swallowed. "Send him up, will you?"

It was another man, all right, but that was about the only difference. He had the same massive build; the same immense dignity. And the conversation ran along almost identical lines. "Good evening, Mr. Clifford . . . A Merry Christmas . . . liberty of offering you a small gift . . . hope you will not find it unacceptable . . ." Another troupe of coolies emerged, deposited their loads and padded morosely away. Whisky, gin, Christmas puddings . . . My thanks were as inadequate as before. No, he didn't drink. No, he wouldn't smoke . . . Barely ten minutes later and he had bowed himself out, leaving me slightly dazed and disbelieving. If it hadn't been for the sight of the crates spread like stepping-stones across the floor I might have suspected that I was in for a bout of fever and had dreamed the whole thing up.

Naïvely, perhaps, I told the house-boy to apologise for my absence in the event of anyone else calling. Then I drove off to my dinner engagement. Hobbs was one of the guests and I took the opportunity of mentioning what had happened. It didn't seem to worry him.

"You've got to watch out for the odd bribe, of course," he said. "Half of 'em hereabouts have their hands permanently set in the illicit tip position, but at this time of the year you're bound to find yourself on the receiving end from all sorts of people—absolute strangers, very often . . . By the way—what did you get?"

41

I told him. He seemed to find it very funny. "I say," he laughed, addressing himself to the others. "Clifford's just got himself saddled with twenty-four Christmas puddings and enough mince pies to feed the five thousand."

I forgot about it all for the time being. There was much to learn and I was very busy, spending a good deal of each day out on the river visiting local rice mills. On the afternoon of Christmas Eve I'd just returned to the office to start on the paper work when Hobbs called me into his room.

"Look," he said. "Witness my signature, will you? It's the annual contract for the provision of labour for the mill. We put it out for tender every year and this gentleman's"—he waved a hand—"quotation has been accepted for the twelve months starting January 1st."

Standing well back from the other side of the desk was one of the giant Sikhs—and a whole lot of pennies dropped at once. How it was that I hadn't noticed him before I couldn't imagine. And which one it was I couldn't be sure. But there wasn't any doubt from the lofty bow he gave me that we'd met on another occasion, or from the slight washing movement of his clasped hands that he was grateful for the way things had turned out. For a second or two I hesitated angrily, wondering whether I should explain to Hobbs that this was one of my mysterious benefactors. But it seemed tactless to raise the matter there and then. And, anyway, my conscience was quite clear. So I signed, and went indignantly back to my papers and then home.

An hour later I had just finished my shower when the house-boy announced with his normal indifference that there was a Sikh waiting to see me. Steaming slightly I put on a dressing-gown and went out to greet him. Again I wasn't certain which of them it was, though I soon found out.

"Well?"

"Mr. Clifford." The flourish of greeting was even more extravagant than before. "Since our little business arrangement has unfortunately failed to materialise, I have come to—"

42

"Business arrangement?" I cut in. "I don't remember any."

He didn't so much as bat an eyelid. "The goods from the cold store in Rangoon, Mr. Clifford."

"I was under the impression they were to do with Christmas. My 'great Christian festival'—remember?"

He made the concession of spreading his hands. "I only imagined that you would prefer to receive them in that spirit. I am sorry if there has been some misunderstanding." He paused. "In the circumstances I should like to collect them. My men are waiting downstairs."

Yes, I said, flabbergasted, he could collect them. At once. The sooner the better. I didn't want to keep the crates in the house a moment longer. I was appalled at the deception, I said, and wanted to make it quite clear that to my way of thinking bribery was a stinking business . . . I said a lot more in the iciest tone I could manage and even helped load up the squad of coolies myself, so anxious was I to let him see that I was disgusted with the whole affair . . .

Later that evening my boy brought me a note. The written English, too, was impeccable; the style rigid with dignity.

Dear Mr. Clifford,

I am most grieved to learn from a friend of mine that you consider the Christmas gifts I brought you the other night were bribes, intended, apparently, to influence the awarding of the mill labour contract. This assertion, you will appreciate, is a reflection on my integrity and good name, particularly since it was my quotation which was fortunate enough to be accepted. I have no alternative therefore but to ask you to return the cold store supplies now at your bungalow. Believe me, it saddens me to do this but I see no alternative.

It only remains for me to wish you a Merry Christmas . . .

As I said at the beginning—I was green then; about as green as could be.

Backwater

WYMAN CUT THE engine and brought the launch round in a tight circle. He had judged it about right; a shade too fine perhaps but, he complimented himself, near enough for an amateur. As they bumped against the rickety jetty a half-naked Indian stretched out a spindly arm and grabbed at the line thrown by the *serang*.

"Keep her here," Wyman said. "There's enough water and I'll be back in half an hour."

He ducked under the awning and, as the launch rocked to a standstill, clambered on to the jetty. There was no breeze and the air was heavy with the stench which rose from the black, glistening mud above the water-line. The heat engulfed him and he caught his breath sharply as the sweat ran from the inflamed pores on his shoulders and forearms. He glanced quickly at the note Thornton had given him the previous evening, then took a look at the mill.

Half-way along the jetty a pi dog, grotesque and almost hairless, lay curled against a pile of rotting sacks. Apart from the dog and the Indian making the rope fast there was no sign of life. The whole place seemed deserted, and the only sound came from the water lapping against the battered piles below. High over the mill three vultures floated silently in a sky drained of colour by the violence of the heat, and along the river bank the palm trees drooped their heads as if from exhaustion.

"God!" Wyman exclaimed softly. "What a hole!"

The mill was not working. There were four bays, with a *godown* at the far end, and the whole structure was a crazy patchwork of corrugated iron sheets and bamboo extending for about thirty yards on either side of the jetty. A path led through the long grass and disappeared behind the *godown*, and above the dilapidated rooftops a rusty chimney reached unsteadily into the still air.

He turned to the Indian crouched near him. "Where is the bungalow?" he asked.

The man looked up, tired eyes sunk deep in their sockets, and pointed listlessly. "That way, sahib; behind the mill. The path will take you."

Wyman walked along the jetty, past the sleeping pi dog, and made his way towards the *godown*. Dry rice husks crackled underfoot at every step and the yellow-brown grass overhanging the path scraped roughly against his khaki drill trousers. The doors of the *godown* were open but he did not stop to go inside, contenting himself with a quick glance into the shadowy interior as he walked by. He would be going there later with Choon Ling. Right now he wanted to meet him and talk things over—and if there was a drink to be had he would be glad of it.

The bungalow was tucked in amongst a few trees immediately behind the *godown*. It was quite large and could have been made to look attractive, but someone had stained the walls a sombre brown and made a bad job of the mottled red roof. Like the mill it was badly in need of repair and the small garden in which it stood was equally unkempt and overgrown. Wyman pushed open the bamboo gate and went slowly past the untended riot of hibiscus, poinsettia and laburnum towards the flight of stairs beneath the building which led up to the floor level. He was beginning to think there was nobody at home; indeed, there had been scarcely any indication that the place was inhabited, but a face

46

appeared suddenly at the open window just above and a voice greeted him cheerfully.

"Hallo there. Mr. Wyman?"

He was surprised at the excellence of the accent. "That's right."

"Come on up."

He climbed the stairs slowly, stumbling a little in the apparent darkness which greeted him after the glare outside, to find a slight young man in an open-necked tennis shirt and grey flannels waiting at the top.

"Sorry I wasn't at the jetty," the Chinaman said as they shook hands. "I didn't know what time to expect you."

"I came when I could. Mr. Thornton mentioned it only last night." Wyman mopped his face with a handkerchief. "This place takes some finding."

Choon Ling smiled. "You're right. It's a bit of a backwater."

He motioned Wyman to sit down. "Would you care for a drink?" he asked; then, without waiting for an answer, added quickly, "I can see you would. Excuse me a minute and I'll bring it in."

"Thank you," Wyman said gratefully.

"Beer?"

"Please. Lovely cold beer."

The young man disappeared into another room and the coloured bead curtain hanging across the doorway clattered for a moment as it swung behind him. Wyman stuffed a damp handkerchief into his hip pocket and leaned back in the cane chair, wincing a little as his shirt pressed against the prickly heat across his shoulders. It was a minute or two before Choon Ling returned and he had time to look about him. The room was sparsely furnished: a few chairs, a low circular table set in the centre, a rush mat or two and a large faded colour print in a heavy frame on the wall opposite—that was about all. It was not unlike other rooms in which Wyman had found himself during the last few weeks, doing business over a glass of beer with one or another of the smaller rice-millers, yet

47

there was something about it which was different . . . and hard to account for. It was not just the dust, or the drabness of the simple furnishings, or the smell of the stale, hot air— they were common enough in places of this sort. There was more to it than that; more than the obvious signs of neglect and decay which had greeted him on the jetty when he first looked at the mill . . . an atmosphere rather than the mere visible evidence of deterioration. But whatever it was defied analysis.

He heard the door of the ice box slam to and the cheerful clink of glasses on a tray, and his tongue ran over his parched lips in unconscious anticipation. The bead curtain clattered again as Choon Ling backed through it into the room and a startled lizard, dozing on the discoloured wall above the door, darted swiftly into a corner for safety.

"Lovely cold beer," Choon Ling said with a smile. "Just what the doctor ordered."

"You shouldn't have bothered."

"No bother at all. I know what it's like when you've been out in that sun for a few hours. Here; take this."

Wyman reached forward and took the long cool glass from the Chinaman's outstretched hand. "Thanks . . . and here's luck."

Choon Ling perched himself on the edge of the table in the centre of the room and nodded appreciatively as he sipped at his beer.

"Down the hatch," he said.

Wyman never claimed to be much good at guessing a person's age but he reckoned his host was somewhere about twenty-eight. A year or so younger maybe, but it was difficult to be sure. You never can tell with the Chinese anyhow, he thought; they always seem to be either young or very old, and apparently move from one state to the other without the necessity of middle age. No doubt it would be the same with Choon Ling. In twenty years' time his round, almost chubby, cheeks would become suddenly lined and drawn, and his sleek, black hair would grow wispy and lose its lustre. Only his

48

eyes, sunken a little above the high cheekbones, would perhaps retain the same curious quality of melancholy that Wyman observed in them now.

"About the rice," Choon Ling began. "I suppose Mr. Thornton gave you the details?"

Wyman nodded and felt for Thornton's note in his breast pocket. "I've got the particulars here somewhere. Sixty tons of Number Two quality I believe he said it was . . ."

"That's right. It's all bagged up, ten to the ton, and ready when you want it." The young man hesitated for a second, then grinned. "*If* you want it, that is."

"I dare say we shall, but you'll understand I can't commit myself until I've seen it and taken a sample. There's a lot of bad stuff about these days—no offence meant, of course— and one has to be careful."

"Naturally. It's for you to decide. We'll go down to the mill just as soon as you say the word. Meanwhile, what about the other half—or are you in a hurry?"

Wyman was in no mood to refuse. There were no more calls to be made that afternoon and he was grateful for the hospitality and the temporary escape from the inferno outside. Besides, he was curious to discover how the young Chinaman had come by his faultless accent and extensive vocabulary, which were a long way removed from the comic commercial brand of English he had grown accustomed to in recent weeks.

As he handed over his empty glass he remarked casually: "I must congratulate you on your English. It's really excellent. I shouldn't have thought you'd have much opportunity for using it out here."

Choon Ling stopped pouring the beer and laughed. "I'm glad you find it so good. I don't use it as much as I would like, for this is a lonely spot and visitors are few and far between. But I speak it better than my native tongue—as indeed I should, for I was ten years in England"—he made a small gesture—"and at Cambridge for three."

Wyman could have kicked himself. There was silence for a

moment as Choon Ling leaned across to give him his glass.

"There is another reason," he continued quietly. "The best reason of all perhaps. I married an English girl."

He must have noticed the look of surprise on Wyman's face. "You didn't know?"

Wyman shook his head.

"I thought everybody knew." There was no bitterness in the way it was said, but he turned his head away as he spoke as if he were afraid his expression might reveal what his voice had managed to hide.

"I haven't been in the area very long," Wyman explained, then cursed himself for being a tactless fool. But Choon Ling did not appear to have noticed the remark. He had moved over to the other side of the room and was staring out of the window, legs astride, hands thrust deep into trouser pockets.

"It's a simple enough story," he said suddenly. "You'll hear it from someone or other before long so I might as well tell you myself." He half turned and looked at Wyman. "If you're interested, of course . . ."

Wyman did not know how to reply. The conversation had taken an unexpected turn and he felt uncomfortably like an eavesdropper who is discovered and invited in so that he can hear everything more clearly. He shifted awkwardly in his chair, and, after a moment's uncertainty, said: "I'd be glad to know. Please go on," and he could tell from the look on the other's face that it was the answer he wanted.

"This mill used to be very prosperous," Choon Ling began. "My father built it about thirty years ago and made a good deal of money. I was the only child and when I was eleven I was sent to school in England. I came home for a few months before going up to the University, but that was my only contact with my family and this place in the whole ten years. When I finally returned it was not of my choosing—my mother had died suddenly and my father had a stroke shortly afterwards. It was my duty to come back and manage things here. Otherwise I should not have come, for apart from my family I had no ties."

50

He paused for a few seconds and then, as if trying to convince himself that he had been right, added firmly, "It was my duty to return. My father had built this business from nothing—someone had to carry on."

Wyman was watching him closely. There were no dramatics, no apparent signs of emotion, but for all that he could tell that the young man was speaking under some kind of strain. Yet he no longer felt embarrassed at intruding into another person's affairs. This story had been bottled up for a long time and he knew he was being used as a safety valve.

"My wife came back with me," Choon Ling went on, still speaking in the same rather flat monotone. "I had met her during my last year at Cambridge—she was a waitress in a London restaurant—and we married not long afterwards. Three months later we left England and came here."

He seemed suddenly unsure of himself. He hesitated before going on and then, looking straight at Wyman, said with great earnestness, "My wife was very beautiful and I was very much in love with her. But she was not prepared for this place. She wanted colour and excitement and laughter in her life, but she could not find it here . . . she said she would go mad if she stayed."

For a moment Wyman thought the unemotional façade was going to crack, but the young man managed to keep control of himself. He turned away towards the window again. "She left here within six months of our arrival. I did all I could to make her contented, but it was no use. I didn't have a chance in a place like this."

"Did you never think of going with her?"

"Many times; but I felt I had to stay here. Rightly or wrongly I thought it my duty. It was not an easy decision to make."

Wyman finished off his beer and got to his feet. "When did this happen?"

"Eighteen months ago." He made a great effort to smile. "I must apologise for bothering you with my troubles. Now we'll get along and look at that rice."

He picked up a battered topee and pulled back the bead curtain for them to pass through. "This is the quicker way," he said. "Down the back stairs."

Wyman found himself in a narrow corridor leading into what seemed to be a kitchen. The passage was quite bare of furniture and the only colour was provided by some heavy curtains screening another doorway which led off to the right. Choon Ling stopped as they were passing it. "This was my wife's room. I hoped it would make her feel more at home. I should like you to see it . . . it will not take a minute."

Wyman was quite unprepared for the scene which greeted him. When he thought about it afterwards he told himself that he ought to have guessed that something of the kind lay hidden behind the faded blue curtains, but now, standing just inside the doorway he found it hard to believe what he saw. For this was not the room of a Chinese rice-miller in a half-forgotten backwater. This was an English drawing room—well carpeted, cosily furnished and tastefully decorated—a room that, at first glance, gave Wyman a momentary feeling of nostalgia. But it was more than just a room. It was, at the same time, both a symbol of a lonely young man's endeavour to keep his wife and a memorial to her having existed.

Choon Ling had entered and was standing beside him. "I haven't touched anything since she left," he said. "It's just as it was when she was here."

He need not have spoken. Everything was in its place, the silver polished, woodwork dusted and shining, fresh flowers on the centre table. Here, at least, there had been no neglect, no letting things slide and decay.

Wyman felt he should say something. "It's a fine room," was all he could manage.

"I'm glad you think so." A pause, then: "Perhaps, one day, she will come back to it." The Chinaman lifted the lid of the gramophone and turned the handle a few times. "Mr. Wyman," he said suddenly. "Have you ever been in love?"

Wyman nodded, but did not reply.

"Then perhaps you will understand." There was a click as

52

the turntable started spinning, and the needle grated roughly on the worn record. "This was my wife's favourite piece of music . . . You will probably think it an ironic choice in the circumstances."

Wyman leaned against the wall and listened as the saccharin-sweet strains of Puccini's "One Fine Day" flooded into the room. Choon Ling was standing with his back to the gramophone but Wyman could see his face in the mirror opposite the door. He was staring at a framed photograph of a not unattractive fair-haired girl who smiled pleasantly in their direction. So that was his wife, Wyman thought, and found himself wondering what her name was and what had become of her.

Then, suddenly, he felt he could stand it no longer. He moved quietly out of the room and went down the back stairs, hardly noticing the stinging pain of the prickly heat when the sun hit him. As he walked along the path towards the bamboo gate he could hear the music rising majestically to its final climax, and it was not until he was rounding the corner of the *godown* that he was free of it altogether.

He had no difficulty in finding the rice. There was only one stack and he broke open a few of the bags and ran the white grains through his fingers. It did not need a detailed examination to see that the quality was poor and that it had suffered from bad milling. He spent perhaps five minutes selecting an occasional bag for a brief inspection, then made a note on the crumpled paper Thornton had given him the day before.

When he got to the door Choon Ling was coming down the path from the bungalow. He looked pale and drawn and, as he drew near, Wyman said, "I've had a look at it. The bagging's all right but there's a proportion of broken grains. When was it milled?"

"Two weeks ago." He was finding it difficult to look Wyman in the face. He swallowed hard and said: "I let everything go when my wife left. The mill hadn't been turned over for more than a year. I got sixty tons out of it last month—then it broke down . . . It was pretty disheartening after making the effort."

They walked in silence down to the jetty, neither of them at ease, the incident in the bungalow hanging like a barrier between them.

Wyman could not bring himself to say what was uppermost in his mind. Instead he asked: "Will you be starting up again soon?"

"I hope so. In a week or two with any luck."

The pi dog was still sleeping by the pile of old sacks and the Indian, crouching at the end of the jetty, rose stiffly to his feet as they approached. Wyman turned to Choon Ling and said, "Mr. Thornton will let you know about the rice . . . I'll be seeing him in the morning, so there won't be any delay."

"Thank you." They shook hands and he went on, "I must apologise for what happened just now . . ."

"Forget it," Wyman broke in quickly. He dropped heavily into the launch and the *serang* started the engine. As they drew away from the jetty the Chinaman called out: "Did you remember to take a sample?" and Wyman avoided answering by pointing to the engine hatch, pretending he could not hear.

There had been no necessity to take a sample, for it was as clear as could be that the rice was below standard. But he felt there was something he ought to do to help, and even before he'd reached the *godown* he had decided to tell Thornton to accept the stuff. It was a nuisance, though, that the quality was so poor, for it might prove awkward for him later on. But he had made up his mind now and was prepared to take the risk.

When he looked back Choon Ling was still waving from the jetty, a small, lonely, tragic figure, and Wyman flapped his handkerchief in acknowledgment until the trees slid between them and the mill was lost to view. He wiped the sweat away from his face and neck and, loud enough for the uncomprehending *serang* to turn his head and stare at him, swore irritably: "To hell with women! Why do they always have to make everything so damned complicated?"

A Matter of Opinion

THE COMMISSIONER PAUSED for a moment. For the first time since the interview began he stopped drumming his fingers on the glass-topped desk.

"I trust I've made myself clear?"

I nodded. "Quite, sir."

"You had no right to act in the way you did," the high-pitched, staccato voice went on remorselessly. "But so long as you realise you exceeded your authority I'm prepared to overlook it . . . You're a young man and you've obviously still a lot to learn." The fingers renewed their drumming. "Don't let it happen again. I may not be able to view the matter as sympathetically another time."

I wanted to tell the bald-headed, ascetic-faced martinet on the other side of the desk how much I hated him. In six months there had never been one word of praise or encouragement—nothing but complaints and reprimands and pettiness, week after week. Ten days ago I hadn't shown enough initiative; now I'd shown too much. Indignation and despair welled up inside me, but I managed to control myself.

"Will that be all, sir?"

"Yes, thank you."

I turned and made my way across the room. As I reached the door the Commissioner spoke again. "One of these days,

Clifford, when you've had thirty years' experience and perhaps occupy this very chair, you'll understand more fully the importance of having an Assistant who knows where his duties begin . . . and end. Right now it will pay you to concentrate on the responsibilities of your present appointment and not to imagine you can anticipate events."

For a second I stared at the man, dumbfounded, then opened the door and went into the outer office. Shaking with fury, I paced up and down in front of the open windows until my anger subsided sufficiently for me to collect my thoughts. It was monstrous, of course; the whole thing was monstrous—and so ruddy unfair! Friends had warned me that the Commissioner was quite impossible and had never kept an Assistant for more than eighteen months at the outside. Up to now I'd been prepared to give him the benefit of the doubt, much as I disliked him. But not any longer; not after that last taunt.

I grabbed my topee from the rack and marched down the corridor leading to the garage. The Burmese sentry on duty at the side door saluted as I stepped outside, then doubled across the lawn to open the gates at the bottom of the drive. I got into the car and deliberately revved the engine two or three times before driving off. The garage was under the private office window and I knew the Commissioner wouldn't like it.

Although twenty-four hours had passed since I left the office, my anger had not entirely disappeared. Every now and then it bubbled up with renewed vehemence. It was whilst in the grip of such a mood that I had suddenly decided to get away on an immediate tour of the local hill districts. Anywhere, I had told myself savagely, anywhere would do, so long as I could avoid the man's company for a few days.

We had been on the move since morning and my thoughts had returned to the incident a dozen times during the journey. But now, as our small party laboriously made its way up the last five hundred feet to the rest house at the top of the escarpment, I was only conscious of fatigue and a nagging pain in my left foot.

It was hard going, with the narrow path made more treacherous by an hour's heavy rain at mid-day. The monsoon was threatening to break early and these sudden preliminary downpours, an unexpected discomfort, had brought out the leeches. They were everywhere, small, writhing black cylinders, reaching down from the overhanging creepers and bamboos and rearing up from the mud on the path itself. Every hour, when we rested, I examined my clothes and the more accessible parts of my body and never found less than a score of them, working their way through to my flesh or with their heads already embedded in my skin. A touch with a lighted cigarette-end and they squirmed away, dropping to the ground to be squelched under my heel, filling me with revulsion and disgust.

The pain in my foot increased rapidly. On the way up I imagined that the instep must be bruised. But when, late in the afternoon, we reached the rest house and I took off my boot and saw the bloated finger-thick leech I realised at once that poison had set in. By six o'clock, when my bearer lit the oil lamp and started fixing the mosquito-net over the bed, I was reduced to hobbling miserably about the room. Half an hour later I was unable to put the foot to the floor. I bathed it in a solution of potassium permanganate and covered it with iodine, but the limitations of the medicine box were soon exhausted and the poison was rapidly taking hold. Already the inflammation had spread as far as the ankle and I knew that the chances of moving on in the morning were dwindling fast.

I called my bearer, but there was no reply. A minute or two later I called a second time, but again there was no response. I was beginning to wonder if I could get to the verandah and shout down to the servants' quarters on the edge of the compound when Maung Hla padded silently into the room.

"Where on earth have you been?"

"To the village, *thakin*."

"A fine time to start roving. Before you go looking at the girls I should like something to drink."

He came over to the side of the bed. "There is a man in the village who can make your foot well," he said. "Will you see him? I have brought him with me."

"What sort of man?"

"Just a man." Maung Hla shrugged. "An old man. He is well known in the area."

"All right," I said. "Send him up—and bring some whisky. I don't feel like eating."

Maung Hla withdrew, returning a moment later with the old villager, a dishevelled, doubled-up gnome, who bowed in greeting before shambling across the room. As he neared the bed and entered the circle of light from the hurricane lamp I saw him more clearly, and grew suddenly apprehensive about what I was letting myself in for. Not for a long time had I seen such an unpleasant-looking character.

The ancient one bowed again. "The *thakin* has a bad foot?"

"That is so."

"I should like to see it."

I fought down a desire to tell him to go away. "All right," I said briefly, and watched suspiciously as the old man prodded and pressed the inflamed flesh with his filthy, gnarled fingers. It hurt like mad, and I screwed up my eyes with the pain.

"It was a leech bite," my tormentor said firmly.

"I am aware of that," I replied, trying not to show my impatience.

"And the *thakin* wishes to travel in the morning?"

I nodded.

The old man scratched the end of his nose and mumbled something I did not understand. Then he said: "If the *thakin* wishes it shall be arranged. But I will need an hour to make the necessary preparations—"

"I will not allow you to use a knife or cut my leg in any way," I broke in. "If that must be done I shall wait until I can get to hospital."

"I shall not cut your leg," the villainous-looking one said. "I shall treat it with jungle herbs—that is all."

I thought about it for a minute. "Very well, then," I said. "Come back when you are ready. It is important that I leave here tomorrow."

"That will present no difficulty, *thakin*."

"You are very certain. At the moment I cannot put the foot to the ground."

"I have much experience. Many years ago the Commissioner *thakin* had a bad leg in another village not far from here. I mended it for him, just as I shall mend yours."

Despite the pain I could not suppress a chuckle. "I hope it hurt," I said without thinking.

"*Thakin?*"

"I said that I was in good company . . . Now, make your preparations and come back quickly."

The hillman returned before nine o'clock and set to work with Maung Hla acting as his assistant. His equipment was simplicity itself—banana leaves, strips of cane, a handful of feathers and a bamboo container filled with thick green liquid. Maung Hla spread a groundsheet across the bed and the old man, crooning quietly, began smearing the vile-smelling liquid over my foot, using the feathers as a crude brush. Within a quarter of an hour my leg was encased in banana leaves almost up to the knee and fastened with the cane strips.

Only once during the whole operation did anyone speak. That was when I pointed to the container and asked: "What is that green stuff made from?"

"That is a secret, *thakin*."

"Well, tell me some of the non-secret things you put in it."

The gnome pondered for a while. "As it is the *thakin* I will tell you," he said at length. "There are jungle leaves, fig juice, monkey blood, chicken droppings . . ."

Wincing at the thought of it, I cut him short and wondered

idly how anyone could collect all these things in less than an hour.

When he'd finished the old man gathered together his equipment and stared at me solemnly. "I shall come in the morning at six o'clock," he announced gravely. "You will find that your foot is quite well when I remove the wrappings."

I felt like saying that I would believe it when I saw it. Instead, I expressed my thanks and told Maung Hla to see that our visitor was well fed before returning to the village. Then, after the ancient had bowed his way to the door, I was left alone. But there was little sleep in store for me. All night unseen devils played with fire inside the casing of banana leaves. Twice I was on the point of tearing them away and plunging the leg into water. And on each occasion, when I thought I couldn't stand any more, the spasm eased sufficiently for me to bear it a while longer. The hours dragged and I lost all sense of time, but towards morning the pain began to lessen and I managed to doze a little.

When I awoke Maung Hla was at the bedside and the hillman was already cutting the strips of cane and peeling off the leaves.

"It does not hurt now, *thakin*?"

"No," I said, surprised. "No, it doesn't. But during the night I thought I was going to die."

They washed the leg clean and I was astonished to find that, apart from some puffiness near the toes, the foot showed no sign of the poison. I got off the bed and tried it gently on the floor. It was a little tender, but I could walk without difficulty.

I turned delightedly to the old man. "I am very grateful to you," I smiled. "You have done me a great service." I was trying to calculate what to offer in payment. It was always a difficult thing to decide. "Were you well fed last evening?"

"Yes, *thakin*."

"Good." I held out a ten rupee note. If anything, I reckoned I was erring on the generous side. "This is for your trouble."

The old man spoke with dignity. "When I mended the Commissioner *thakin's* leg he paid me fifteen rupees. And his leg was not as bad as yours."

"But I am not the Commissioner," I said. "The Commissioner is a big man; of much greater importance. It was right that he should have paid you more."

"That is not so, *thakin*," the other insisted. "The Commissioner may be a big man, but on that occasion he did not behave like one. He caused a great deal of trouble and, as I have said, his leg was not as bad as yours. It is the only time I have met him and I was very disappointed. You have carried yourself much more as I expected a Commissioner should."

For one mad, happy moment I felt that I loved the dirty, bent villager more than I had ever loved anyone in my life. With an impulsive gesture I thrust twenty rupees into his hand. The Commissioner was bound to query the item when he examined the expense account, and the opportunity would be there to explain the whole matter in detail. And that, I had already decided, was exactly what I was going to do.

Cost Price

In a small station like Mansein, where almost everything you did was common knowledge within a few hours, the dozen or so Europeans who met in the Club each evening or—by way of variation—asked a few people (in strict rotation) to dinner at their bungalows, had learned to be charitable. It was, after all, only prudent not to take violent exception to the faults and lapses of others when, after a hard day up at the mill or on the river, it may be that you hit the bottle too heavily yourself and behaved not quite as well as you should have done.

By this I do not mean that our way of living was any worse than other isolated white communities in Burma—far from it. Toleration of the other person's idiosyncrasies was an absolute necessity if the dangerously thin veneer of our social life was to remain unbroken, and I suppose at times we all got away with rather more than we should have done in different circumstances.

There was a limit, however, to this mutually-evolved code, and Carson had long since ceased to be subject to it. Nobody liked Carson, and if ever a man deserved unpopularity it was this heavily-built, middle-aged Australian river pilot who, for ten years or more, had taken the occasional cargo steamers up and down between the rice mill and the sea.

It was a difficult feat, and it required a clear head and a good deal of skill to negotiate an 8,000 tonner through the contorted, labyrinthine channels of the river delta. When he first came to Mansein there was no doubt that Carson possessed both qualities in sufficient measure to warrant his being acknowledged a first-rate pilot, but they had long since deserted him. Ten years of almost continuous debauchery had taken their toll, and he'd been warned by his superiors on more than one occasion that he would have to pull himself together.

At first, despite his excessive predilection for the bottle and a delight in verbal obscenities which were an embarrassment in mixed company, he was accepted as a useful member of the community. He joined the Club, took part in the social round, and did his job: and although nobody much cared for his company neither did they go out of their way to avoid it. A new face in a small station was always a welcome change, at least until the novelty wore off. And Carson's novelty wore off very quickly.

Within a few months he tried to seduce one of the women and, if it hadn't been that she and her husband were moving almost immediately to another area and wanted to avoid a scandal, I think he would have been finished there and then. But that was only the beginning. It wasn't long before he started borrowing money and, more often than not, the cheques he offered in settlement came back from the bank. People were soon giving him the cold shoulder when he came to the Club, and his invitations to dinner became progressively less frequent until, in the end, they stopped altogether.

Almost anyone else would have long before taken the hint; but not Carson. He had the hide of a rhinoceros and made no effort to change his ways, frequenting the Club whenever it suited him, borrowing from the Indian servants if his luck was out elsewhere, and invariably being pulled home, completely drunk, by rickshaw. Then, some three years back, he'd taken a Burmese girl as his mistress and gone to live in a ramshackle bungalow at the other end of the town. There was some talk about having him barred from the Club, though it came to nothing because it was found he'd been accepted for life membership.

But the sands were running out. Shortly after Christmas he failed to meet a ship at the rendezvous point off the mouth of the river and kept her hanging about for twenty-four hours before he was fit enough, and the tides were right, to bring her up to the mill. He pleaded malaria and his superiors gave him the benefit of the doubt, though they made it quite clear they'd stand no more of it. A couple of months later the skipper of a small coaster judged him incapable of taking charge of his vessel and refused to let him navigate her down river. Carson blustered and swore like a madman at first, but when Hamilton, the Medical Officer, was called, and confirmed that he was quite unfit to be in control of the bridge, he accepted it with sudden docility, finished a bottle of the captain's whisky, and allowed himself to be assisted off the ship.

That was the end, and he knew it. A new man, who'd had some experience on the river when Carson had been on short leave, was flown over from Rangoon, took the ship down next day, and relieved Carson of his duties forthwith. None of us was sorry. We had all seen it coming and had been hoping it might have happened a good deal earlier than it did.

I told Oliver about all this—and a good deal more besides —when he dined with me one night at my bungalow. During recent years the volume and scope of my work had increased enormously, and I had for some time past been badgering Head Office to send me an assistant out from home. I could have asked for someone to be transferred from another part of Burma, but my mind was set on getting a person whom I could train in my own way, so that, when I was on furlough, I shouldn't be worrying my head about how affairs were being conducted in my absence.

Oliver arrived a month before the rains, at the peak of the hot weather, and so got off to about the most uncomfortable start a newcomer could possibly have. But he made light of it and set about learning the work with a quiet enthusiasm that delighted me. I took him out on the river as much as possible during his first two or three weeks, so that he could see the extent of the area for which we were responsible and meet some of the native rice-millers in the more out-of-the-way backwaters. To have started him off on long hours of office work, and expected him to concentrate with the thermometer as high as it was, would have been asking too much; and, in any case, it was a good thing to get the touring done before the weather broke.

As a result, apart from a couple of visits to the Club and a dinner or two, he had scarcely come into contact with the others. Yet there was no doubt he'd already created an impression. Muriel Burleigh, for instance, had met him at dinner one evening and had shown such an interest in him that even her husband, who had long since resigned himself to the expectant enthusiasm with which she greeted every newcomer to the station, was more than somewhat taken aback. But the District Superintendent of Police, or anyone else for that matter, needn't have worried, for Oliver's amorous intentions were reserved for the girl he'd left behind in England.

He talked about her a good deal when we were out on the river. Not much at first, and with an engaging shyness I found unusual in a young man of twenty-five, but more as the days went by and we got to know each other better. He carried her photograph in his pocket and there was a large, framed portrait of her on the dressing-table up at his bungalow. She was certainly an attractive-looking girl.

One day I asked him: "When are you going to marry her?"

He grinned, and said: "Next year, with luck."

"What's luck got to do with it? Don't you think she'll come out?"

"She'll come, all right," he replied. "It's just that I've got to make a go of this job first."

I liked him for that. "Don't you worry," I said. "You'll make a go of it—you've got the best incentive in the world. Now, you see that mill over on the far bank . . ." and we were back at work again.

It was a few days after Carson was dismissed that I asked Oliver to dine with me and told him the whole story. He'd been along on several other occasions, mostly in the evenings, but much of the time had been spent introducing him to the administrative side of his job, for it was cooler and more pleasant to do so at the bungalow, with a whisky or two to help us along, than in the hot-house of an office at the back of the mill. But, not wishing to drive him too hard, and with the rains due at any moment, I thought it was about time he eased off a bit and began taking a more active part in the limited, but highly-geared, social life of the station.

So that night I gave him half a dozen verbal sketches of the people he hadn't yet met, refreshed his memory about the others and, as best I could, told him a little about the subtleties of successful living in such a small community.

He listened attentively; laughed now and then when I came out with a particularly outrageous anecdote about somebody or other, and asked a few questions. I left Carson to the last, and when I had finished Oliver was silent for a while.

Then he said, "What's going to happen to the girl?"

For a moment I didn't quite follow. "What girl?"

"The one who's been living with Carson."

"I've no idea," I said. "I suppose she'll go back to her village, though—quite honestly—I hadn't given it a thought."

He nodded, and began talking about something else. After a while I suggested we drive over to the Club for a couple of hours, so we finished our drinks and went downstairs to the car. It was warm enough indoors with all the fans going, but outside it was like a furnace. I drove fast under the wide scatter of stars, with the moonlight turning the billowing train of dust behind us into silver, and the night air pushing hot and heavy against our faces. Away to the south-west the clouds were massing and piling up in the sky in readiness for the approaching storm.

It took us only a few minutes to reach the Club and I parked the car in the dark shadows of the tamarinds at the far end of the compound.

Only four others were there when we went in—the Commissioner and his wife, Burleigh and Hamilton—sitting in a small group under the largest fan near the bar. Oliver had met them all on a previous occasion so introductions were unnecessary, and we pulled our chairs over to join their circle.

"Hardly a full house tonight," I said.

"N-not to be wondered at," Burleigh stuttered. "We've an unexpected visitor. The others have g-gone as a result."

"Carson?"

Hamilton nodded.

"I thought we'd seen the last of him."

"Nearly, but not quite," Burleigh said. "He's leaving t-tomorrow."

I signed the chit for our drinks and looked round the room. There was a half-filled glass of whisky and a tin of cigarettes on the table in the corner. "Where is he?" I asked.

"Outside," the Commissioner's wife said. "And when he comes back, if you'll excuse us, we're leaving."

Carson shambled in from the verandah as she spoke and made his way unsteadily to the far table. He was very drunk and called in a raucous voice to the bearer for more whisky. I could see that Oliver was watching him closely.

The Commissioner touched his wife's arm. "Ready when you are."

She nodded, and we all rose to our feet together.

"Good night," she said, smiling at us in turn. "And don't forget, Mr. Oliver, that you're dining with us on Wednesday."

"I'm looking forward to it."

They were nearly at the door when Carson started to laugh; a deep-throated, gurgling sort of chuckle which I had come to hate. "I'm afraid I shan't be there," he roared. "Otherwise engaged." The Commissioner made as if to say something, checked himself, and followed his wife outside. Carson stared after them and went on shaking with laughter.

Under the yellow light of the overhead lamp his blotched,

contorted face looked the very personification of evil. He half sprawled across the table, and, as his amusement subsided, his small inflamed eyes settled on us with sullen indifference. It must have been some days since he'd shaved, and his khaki shirt and shorts were crumpled and stained with sweat patches.

"Bitch!" he said suddenly. "—— bitch!"

Burleigh was furious. "K-keep your remarks t-to yourself, C-Carson," he shouted angrily. "Or g-get out!"

Carson waved a hand, as if in greeting. "Keep your shirt on, old boy," he said. "Don't let's have any trouble on my last night." He chuckled again. "Mustn't have any unpleasant memories to take away with me."

He shouted for another whisky and staggered over to where we were sitting. "Off to Rangoon in the morning," he announced hoarsely. "Three months' pay and a passage home—that's all the ——'s have given me after ten years in this God-forsaken hole." His fist crashed down on the table. "Mean swine; mean bloody swine!"

Nobody said anything. Carson was slumped in the chair next to Oliver and I was suddenly conscious of the contrast the two of them presented—the fair-haired, rather earnest young man with a newly-acquired tan not yet burned deep into his skin, and the degenerate, uncouth figure at his side.

Carson seemed to notice him for the first time. "Don't know you," he said, peering with blood-shot eyes. "New boy?"

I thought I ought to say something. "Mr. Oliver is my new assistant."

Carson belched quietly. "How long've you been here?"

"Nearly a month," Oliver said.

"A month?" The drunken man laughed. "Wait till you've been here ten bloody years . . . You'll wish you'd never set eyes on the place."

Hamilton, who'd hardly said a word since we arrived, stubbed his cigarette out and started to get up. "Think I'll push off now," he said awkwardly. "Early to bed, and all that . . ."

69

Carson lurched forward in his chair. "Wait a minute, doc," he rasped. "Before you go, what about doing me a favour?"

The old doctor blinked nervously. "What sort of favour?" he asked cautiously.

"Help me out of a jam." Carson leered up at the other man. ". . . And do yourself a bit o' good at the same time."

"I don't understand."

"You put me on the spot with your blasted report." The words slurred into one another, but there was a note of urgency about them. "There's a Pathan money-lender waiting for me outside and I'll never get clear of the country until I settle with him. I've got to have a thousand rupees, and—"

Burleigh cut in. "Don't listen t-to him, doc."

Carson didn't take his eyes off Hamilton. "It's not a loan this time. Strictly business, and a bargain at the price."

"I still don't understand," Hamilton said.

"If you'll let me have a thousand," Carson said slowly, "you can have my girl Ma Ba Khin."

There wasn't a sound for a moment, and when Hamilton eventually spoke, it was almost a whisper. "You must be mad."

"Not on your life. Cashing in on my last remaining asset, that's all."

Burleigh had gone almost purple. "She's not your p-property," he exploded. "You can't g-go around selling something that isn't yours. Just b-because you're drunk you think you can g-get away with anything. It's a monstrous suggestion, and if you weren't leaving t-tomorrow, I'd—"

"If I wasn't going," Carson said roughly, "I wouldn't be offering her to anyone. She's the best girl I've ever found and at a thousand chips she's a bargain." He transferred his attention to me. "If Hamilton doesn't want her, what about you? I can understand it'd be difficult for Burleigh."

For a second I thought Burleigh was going to strike him. "Nothing doing," I said. "And Burleigh's right—you've no claim on her."

"She's my servant. If nobody wants her here I can still take her over to Rangoon in the morning."

"And what then?"

He drained his glass. "Sell her to one of the houses."

"I always thought you were a swine," I said, as easily as I could. "Now I know."

Hamilton stared at him incredulously. "You're joking."

Carson almost snarled at him. "I'm not. I'm bloody serious, and if no one's interested that's what I'm going to do." He leaned back in the cane chair, and eyed us in turn. "What offers?"

It was Oliver who broke the long silence that followed. For the last few minutes he had been tracing invisible patterns on the glass-topped table with a finger. Now he said quietly, "I'll let you have the money."

We all looked at him, startled. Burleigh and I began to speak but, as if anticipating our protests, he broke in firmly, "I've quite made up my mind." Turning to Carson, he said again, "I'll let you have the money. Are you sure you can't do with less than a thousand?"

Carson sat up, ignoring the question. "When?" was all he said.

"Now, if you like."

"In cash?"

Oliver smiled. "I·don't carry an amount like that about with me. It'll have to be by cheque."

Burleigh groaned.

"A cheque's no good to me. I want cash—if not now, in the morning," Carson insisted.

"It'll be in the morning then," Oliver replied. "Come to my bungalow at ten o'clock and I'll have it ready for you." He paused, and added, almost shyly, "And don't forget to bring the girl with you."

Carson belched with surprise. "The girl? You don't want the girl, do you?"

"Of course. Why else do you think I'm letting you have the money?"

"What d'you want her for?"

"That's my business."

They stared at each other.

"Well, I'll be . . ." Carson said angrily, then suddenly started to laugh. "All right, all right. A bargain's a bargain. I'll be there . . . we'll both be there." And with that he called for another whisky.

I suppose I should have interfered; warned Oliver not to be a fool; perhaps forbidden him to have any dealings with the man. Yet it seemed I had no right to meddle with something which was, after all, a private matter. And, anyhow, I believed he was capable of managing his own affairs. For a youngster he seemed very certain of himself and had handled Carson with remarkable self-assurance.

Any fears I may have had were quickly dispelled on the way home in the car, half an hour later. No sooner had we left the Club than Oliver started to explain. "I hope you didn't mind," he began. "I don't really want the girl, but I couldn't have that swine getting rid of her to a brothel. And if I don't take her he'll probably collect my thousand and sell her anyway."

"After seeing him tonight I think that's very probable," I said. "But what are you going to do with her?" I remembered his question earlier in the evening. "If I were you I'd send her back where she came from."

"I'd thought of that," he said. "But I've decided to keep her. I'll let my bearer train her to be useful about the house so that Joan can have her as a personal servant when she comes out. There's nothing wrong in that, is there?"

"I guess not. It's a rum idea, but it sounds reasonable enough."

"That's what I thought," he said with a grin. "Meanwhile, I'll wait and see what I'm getting for my money."

I dropped him off at his bungalow and drove home, my mind full of the evening's events. I drove slowly, and watched the lightning flap gently amongst the blue-black clouds along the horizon.

The rains came the following afternoon, with all their cus-

72

tomary fury, and the parched earth quickly swallowed up the preliminary downpours. After a week or two it had had its fill, but still did its best to cope with the onslaught. A green stain spread quickly over the flat countryside, pools and paddy-fields filled with water and the frogs started their nightly, hoarse-throated chorus; the temperature dropped about fifteen degrees, dirt roads were churned into strips of mud and, at long last, my prickly heat disappeared.

It was the same every year and, once the prelude was over, we settled down to the long-drawn monotony that was to be our lot for the next six months. The life of the station closed in, and we became even more dependent on one another's company. The news about Carson's last night had spread quickly and, for a time, Oliver was the subject of a good deal of banter wherever he went, particularly from the women, whose curiosity often outweighed their sense of fun. Many young men might have resented it, but Oliver remained unruffled and even referred to the incident himself on occasions.

The weeks dragged by. Oliver was proving invaluable and, as his experience and knowledge of the language increased, I found myself able to off-load more of my work on to his shoulders. I was up at his bungalow fairly frequently during this period and, once or twice, caught sight of Carson's girl busying herself about the house under the watchful eye of Oliver's bearer.

The Burmese women have a rare quality of beauty that is all their own, and Ma Ba Khin was well-endowed with it. She was, I guessed, about twenty, and if, perhaps, her face was a little too flat for perfection, her figure and bearing were more than adequate compensation. But what I remember most clearly, was the extraordinary, almost contemptuous, expression of her eyes and the way her mouth curled at the corners as if she were having difficulty in suppressing some particularly malicious joke.

One evening, early in July, there was a breakdown at the

mill which kept me there until nearly midnight. I had been back at the bungalow about a quarter of an hour when the 'phone rang. I half expected it was the Indian mill engineer to say that the thing had gone wrong again, and was surprised to hear Burleigh's voice.

"Did I g-get you out of bed?" He sounded agitated, though you never knew with that stutter.

I told him that I'd just come in and asked what it was he wanted.

"Will you come round t-to my office at once?"

"Your office?"

"Yes, please. It's very urgent."

"Can't you tell me what the trouble is?"

A slight pause, then: "I'd rather n-not, on the 'phone."

"All right," I said. "I'll be there in ten minutes."

On the way over I tried to kid myself it was probably about a theft at the rice store—they were not uncommon—though I knew very well that, if it was, Burleigh would have waited until morning before getting in touch with me. But directly I got there and saw him, tense and drawn, pacing up and down, I knew this was no routine matter.

"Well?" I said.

It seemed a long time before he spoke. "It's about Oliver," he said at last.

"What about him?"

He hesitated for a fraction of a second before replying. "He's d-dead, Bill."

I stared at him incredulously. I'd been prepared for almost anything except that. "Dead?" I echoed stupidly. "Oliver dead?"

Burleigh nodded. His hand was on my arm. "I'm t-terribly sorry. He was found shot a c-couple of hours ago."

"Oh, God! . . . Where?"

"At his bungalow." He leaned across the desk and poured out some whisky. "Here—take this. And s-sit down."

I just stared at him. My brain was leaden and I felt suddenly empty inside.

74

"D-drink it up," Burleigh insisted quietly. "There's a g-good fellow."

I sank into a chair and shut my eyes. "How did it happen?" I heard myself ask.

"Shot-gun," he said gently. "In the head. It m-must have been instantaneous. The g-girl reported it."

The girl! "Carson's girl?"

"Yes."

Desperately I tried to think. My mind went back to the last occasion I had seen Ma Ba Khin, and the memory of the contemptuous look in her eyes and the sardonic curl of her lips made me shudder.

"I'm t-terribly sorry," Burleigh said again. "He was a n-nice boy . . . One of the b-best."

I looked up. "He'd planned to marry at Christmas. Why, in God's name, should he commit suicide?" I thumped my fist on the arm of the chair. "Why, Burleigh, why?"

"It wasn't suicide, Bill," Burleigh answered. "It was m-murder."

"*Murder?*"

"She shot him . . . I've t-taken a statement from her."

It was all coming too fast for me, and I still didn't understand. There seemed to be only one explanation, but I couldn't bring myself to accept it. "He was in love with Joan," I went on doggedly. "I've never known anyone so much in love."

Burleigh came over to where I was sitting. "And Ma Ba Khin loved Carson," he said.

"You can't be serious."

He shrugged his shoulders. "She t-told me so herself, and I've n-no reason to d-disbelieve her."

"But—"

"And she k-killed Oliver because he b-bought her." He lifted the glass from my hand. "She'd have d-done the same to anyone who t-took her away from Carson."

"Is that the only reason?"

"Yes. I know what you're thinking, b-but you're wrong.

75

Oliver n-never so much as t-touched her. She j-just hated him for what he'd d-done. That's all there is to it."

I was too stunned to reply for a moment.

"Love's a f-funny thing, Bill," Burleigh said, but I wasn't really listening. I was thinking of the question Oliver had asked me the night he met Carson—"What's going to happen to the girl?"

I knew the answer now, but it was too late to do anything about it.

Out of the Frying Pan

IT WOULD CERTAINLY be unkind, and probably inaccurate, to say that Betty Garfield was unfaithful to her husband, but it was undoubtedly true that she liked plenty of variety when it came to men. This, however regrettable, would not have presented any serious difficulty in a decent-sized town, but in the half-forgotten, out-of-the-way places Freddie was always being posted to it frequently became a problem of some importance. And for that reason the pair of them had sampled the comforts and discomforts of more stations throughout the length and breadth of Burma than most people managed in the whole of their service. No sooner had Freddie got settled and adjusted himself to local conditions—which took a goodish while, for he was a bit of a plodder—than Betty had exhausted the possibilities of the place. It was all very trying for both of them. Trying for Betty, because she became restless and started badgering him to apply for a transfer; and trying for Freddie, because he hoped one day to grow roots and only renew his acquaintance with the turmoil and inconvenience of packing when they were due for home leave.

They were an odd couple, though well-liked, and had been in Thanbaing for almost two years, which was rather longer than they'd managed anywhere else. This was almost entirely due to the fact that we were a somewhat larger community than most of the others along the Tenasserim coast and, in consequence, Betty had found more to maintain her interest than had been the case for quite a while.

Freddie had long since resigned himself to her continual flirtations and, since I'd known him, seemed prepared to accept them as an inevitable part of the price he must pay for security of tenure in his latest appointment. Indeed, when her interest in young Bradshaw, the Assistant Superintendent of Police, began to wane Freddie showed signs of anxiety that his days in Thanbaing might be numbered. But she soon found somebody else, and the worried look disappeared from Freddie's face.

It was a curious way of going on, particularly as they seemed very fond of each other. At a guess I'd say that Freddie was about fifty, but I'm not much good at people's ages. Betty was considerably younger, though she must have been on the wrong side of forty. She was dark-haired, plump and not in the least good-looking, but possessed of an incredible vitality and a marked sense of humour, which found expression in a permanent twinkle in her eyes and a capacity for a great deal of laughter. There was something undeniably attractive about her.

Freddie was not cast in the same mould, being rather tall and wiry, slow in mind and body, and quite unable to see a joke unless you endured the indignity of explaining it to him afterwards. But for all that he was a pleasant enough person, very sincere and always prepared to go out of his way to lend you a helping hand.

After Bradshaw, Betty fastened on to Hyams, the engineer in charge of the new bridge they were erecting a few miles down river. How far these affairs ever went I wouldn't care to say, but Freddie worried no more about this one than he had over the others. Whenever I went into the European Club he would almost invariably be there, perched on a high stool at the bar, drinking whisky and glancing through the pages of an illustrated paper. And, almost invariably, the conversation would go something like this.

"Evening, Freddie."

"Hallo there. What'll you have?"

"Whisky, please."

A pause while I clambered up beside him. Then, casually: "Seen my wife?"

Sometimes I had, sometimes not. Quite often during that particular cool weather it would be: "Yes, as a matter of fact I have—over at Hyams' place about an hour ago, playing tennis."

"Hyams' place, eh?" he'd say, as if surprised; brood on it for a moment, then add: "Ah, well; keeps her out of mischief, I suppose." And with that he'd go back to his reading.

But one day, early in the New Year, Hyams' star suffered a sudden and complete eclipse with the arrival in Thanbaing of Major Wainwright. Betty transferred her interest to the newcomer lock, stock and barrel, and Hyams was left to concentrate his undivided attention on the esoteric problems inherent in bridge construction.

Blair Wainwright was an extraordinarily handsome man in the middle thirties, with jet-black wavy hair, fine teeth and astonishingly blue eyes. He was blessed with a good physique, carried himself well and sported a moustache of outsize proportions, and Betty Garfield wasn't the only woman in the station to be impressed with the total effect. She was, however, well aware of this fact and, spurred on by the unusual degree of competition, rapidly established an outstanding lead over her rivals. Very soon the others dropped out of the unequal contest, and Betty had Wainwright all to herself.

He enjoyed every minute of it with an air of almost adolescent naïvety, his blue eyes meekly proclaiming a virginal innocence about such matters, as if nothing like it had ever happened to him before. This was a most effective addition to his other attractions and Betty found the combination irresistible. Within a couple of months it was obvious that the affair was getting a bit out of hand. Two or three new faces appeared on the scene, but for once Betty showed no interest in them: she and Wainwright had become quite inseparable.

People had been talking about it for a week or more before Freddie seemed to notice that anything out of the ordinary was going on. When I went into the Club one night he was mounted on his usual seat, staring blankly at the array of bottles behind the bar. I ordered two whiskies and waited for the inevitable question.

"Seen my wife?" he asked.

"Not since this afternoon, Freddie. She was up at the swimming pool."

"Was that chap Wainwright there?"

"Yes, as a matter of fact, he was."

He pushed his hands slowly through his thinning brown hair and grunted indignantly. "Fellow's no good. I've been watching him recently, and I wouldn't trust him further than I could throw him."

And that, for Freddie, was saying a lot.

Early in April I called in at the Club on my way back from the office and was surprised to find him sitting at a table in the corner of the lounge with his wife. Betty was looking very subdued and Freddie, upright in his chair and a bit red in the face, nodded formally as I went over. I guessed they'd been having a row.

"Nice to see you both," I said, as cheerfully as I dared.

"Come and join us," Freddie said. "I've got something to tell you."

"I'd better not, if you don't mind—I'm due at the Robertsons' at seven. What's the news?"

Freddie cleared his throat. "Last month I applied for a transfer," he said firmly.

Betty was showing a sudden interest in the hem of the table-cloth.

I couldn't think of what to say. "I'm sorry," was all I could manage.

"About time we moved on," Freddie continued, painfully forcing a smile. "Don't want to get into a rut, you know."

Someone was crossing the room behind me, and from the way Betty's face suddenly lit up I knew it was Wainwright. He sat down without a word and grinned happily at each of us in turn.

Freddie went red in the face again and said pompously, "I was telling Brown here that I've just learned my application for a transfer to another station has been accepted."

Wainwright leaned forward, blue eyes wide with innocence. "I'm sorry to hear it," he said after a moment's hesitation. "Everyone will miss you. Where are you off to?"

"Mamyo," Freddie said.

"Mamyo!" Wainwright repeated, with polite interest. "It's a nice spot—know it well. As a matter of fact I've got a brother up there—in the Forestry Department." He flicked his moustache and chuckled happily. "Bit of a bounder, my brother—very good-looking chap and rather keen on the women—but I think you'll like him when you get used to him."

It was lucky I was leaving. I saw Freddie's face fall and I could never have stayed there without disgracing myself; but I wasn't sure whether I wanted to laugh or cry.

A Bear Called Priscilla

OUTSIDE OF A ZOO, I've only seen two Himalayan black bears in my life.

The first time was during a leave I spent after the retreat from Burma in 1942. I had gone to Kashmir for a couple of weeks and my companion pointed the bear out to me while we were riding in the hills above Srinagar. It was all of a quarter of a mile away, across a valley, and looked about half an inch high. Somehow, at that distance, it didn't seem a very impressive creature and the occasion was hardly alarming.

However, just a month later, while in Lahore, I saw another. This one was very impressive indeed—so much so that I bought it from its owner, an itinerant beggar who was wandering about with the animal on a length of steel chain. What sudden whim prompted me to possess it I can't imagine. What I paid for it was even then a mystery. The sad truth is that I was rather drunk at the time and didn't begin to appreciate what I had let myself in for until the following morning when my servant woke me and announced that the bear was outside the hotel.

"Bear?" I queried. "What bear?"

"The one you purchased last night, sahib."

"Don't be ridiculous," I said. "Get me the Alka-Seltzer."

I am rarely at my best first thing and that particular morning was the very opposite of an exception. While I bathed and shaved a few preposterous memories stirred, but they seemed as improbable as a dream. And as my servant, with his customary impassive tact, said no more about the matter I was ready to forget all about it.

A bear, indeed! What next?

The hotel manager was in a very different frame of mind. He came over to my table as I was finishing breakfast. In a voice rigid with hauteur, he said: "I am sorry to trouble you, Mr. Clifford, but I should be greatly obliged if you would have your bear taken away as soon as possible."

My heart sank a little. It was true then. A fact. Throughout breakfast the realisation had been dawning. Last night I really had bought a bear.

"Naturally," I said, doing my best to appear unconcerned. "Where is it at the moment?"

"Where you left it, Mr. Clifford." His tone was icy. "Tethered to one of the palm trees by the hotel entrance. It is causing no little inconvenience to our guests."

"I'll see to it right away," I said, continuing to preserve face.

He accompanied me across the lobby and through the swing doors. There he halted, leaving me to go on alone. Several people were standing nervously at the top of the steps and I felt as if I had a gun in my back as I walked past them. The bear was where the manager had said it was—and it looked huge. All too clearly I remembered it from the night before.

Inwardly, I groaned. I hadn't the least idea what I was going to do—then or later. The bear reared up as I approached and did a shuffling sort of dance, reaching out with its arms as if welcoming me as a partner. It had a white crescent across its chest and it stood about five and a half feet high. Despite its size it appeared harmless enough, friendly enough, so I went sufficiently close to be able to chuck it under the chin—just to make it look as though we had been acquainted for years. I felt more foolish than frightened. The bear rested its paws on my shoulders and surveyed me with

84

enormous moist eyes, making small snuffling noises which apparently indicated pleasure.

Emboldened, the manager came a little nearer. "What are you going to do about it, Mr. Clifford?"

"It's a she," I said. I hadn't the slightest idea *what* it was, but if I owned this bear some esoteric knowledge was plainly called for. "Her name's Priscilla," I added on a wild impulse. "Priscilla."

"Really?" The manager was not impressed. "Nevertheless, what are you—?"

"I'm taking her with me, of course." I tapped Priscilla's nose playfully. "We're going back to camp, aren't we, old girl?"

Priscilla repeated her dancing shuffle. The throng on the steps murmured. The manager backed away apprehensively.

"The sooner the better, Mr. Clifford. The sooner the better."

"Don't worry," I said. "We'll be gone by noon."

With as much dignity as I could muster, I led Priscilla from the entrance and tied her under another tree on the far side of the lawn. She gave me no trouble at all. I doubt if there has ever been a tamer, more docile bear. Her claws were non-existent and she didn't even wear a muzzle. Only her size and gregarious disposition made her seem alarming.

It so happened that I had just been posted to an organisation which specialised in parachuting volunteers behind the enemy lines as well as training them in all manner of licensed skulduggery. No regimental soldier could have expected to return from weekend leave with a bear and not find himself in front of the C.O. within minutes of reporting for duty. But the group to which I then belonged was, to say the least, informal. Bizarre, some said. The training-camp mess already possessed a vociferous parrot and a kleptomaniac Rhesus monkey and, thinking quickly, I decided that it could do worse than have Priscilla as well.

I sent a telegram to the adjutant, saying simply: ARRIVING THIS AFTERNOON WITH BLACK BEAR. Then I set about the problem of getting her there. The railway people wouldn't do anything to help and neither would several road-haulage contractors—at least, not at such short notice. Eventually, after protracted telephoning, I came to the conclusion that I would have to take her myself in the jeep.

I wasn't too happy about it, but Priscilla was obviously delighted with the notion. She found the jeep fascinating and rocked it from side to side as if it were a toy before at last sitting in the back where I wanted her. A fair-sized crowd had gathered somewhat sceptically to see us off and I suppose we must have made a rather ridiculous sight. Just as I was about to drive away, the manager, giving the rear of the jeep a wide berth, hurried out to hand me a telegram.

It was from the adjutant and it merely said: PINK, SURELY?

We had about one hundred and fifty miles to go and it took me more than five hours. The initial rush of air excited Priscilla no end and she started bouncing about in a state of high exhilaration. More than once I feared that she would hurl herself into the road. I was therefore forced down to a crawl, which seemed to suit her much better. She squatted behind my back, towering over me, snout raised like a Bisto kid. Not unexpectedly, our passage caused a good deal of consternation along the route. But apart from a short period about half-way when Priscilla became bruisingly affectionate, slapping her heavy paws on my shoulders and nuzzling against my neck—which made it difficult for me to steer a course— the journey was uneventful.

The more I think about that bear, the more splendid are my memories of her. She made a great hit with everyone at the camp with the possible exception of the monkey. The C.O. readily agreed to her becoming the establishment's mascot, and though it very soon became evident that Priscilla was as masculine as could be, the name stuck. We kept her tethered outside the mess and the mess orderlies were deputed to see that she was watered and fed.

During the day we mooched off to our various training

areas and busied ourselves with explosives, unarmed combat and all kinds of uncivilised activities. Whenever we limped over to the mess Priscilla would greet us with her ungainly dance routine and snuffled pleas to come within arms' length. I generally accepted her invitation—as did some of the others—exchanging a few hefty pats before extricating myself from her clutches and withdrawing indoors. There was not the least danger and her appeals were invariably irresistible.

One evening, however, Loader, the unarmed-combat instructor, started to wrestle with her. This happened at our weekly guest night. Because of the nature of our organisation guests were strictly taboo; but that was a mere detail. A guest night was an excuse for a party and we were in need of parties then. The future was far from promising and most of us felt that we were living on borrowed time.

Fired, perhaps, by some deep-rooted frustration, Loader began wrestling with Priscilla after dinner. She accepted the challenge with great amiability. It was an astonishing spectacle, ludicrous, Thurber-esque. Grunting and snuffling, the two of them rolled and stumbled about on the grass and Priscilla seemed to enjoy every minute of it, ponderously countering each excruciating leg-hold, neck-hold and half-Nelson that Loader attempted to apply.

It wasn't long before Loader had had enough. He emerged exhausted but unscathed. But once every week for the next month the contest was resumed—by popular request. Raucously partisan, we used to stand round in a circle and urge them on to more extravagant effort. Priscilla took it all in good part and once or twice even seemed to be endeavouring to emulate some of Loader's professional touches.

This weekly cabaret turn would probably have lasted as long as the war itself. But, alas, one evening the bear disappeared. When Loader went to fetch her all he found was a broken chain and an empty whisky bottle. We searched near and far for hours, but without success. I offered a reward, but to no avail. Clearly, Priscilla had taken to the hills.

Loader was particularly upset; you might have thought that

she was *his* property. Nobody admitted to giving her the whisky but the violence of subsequent unarmed-combat sessions left no doubt that he suspected each and every one of us. Fortunately, about ten days later, the mystery was solved. Paleface, the Rhesus monkey, was observed furtively escaping from a window behind the mess bar, lugging a bottle of gin. A court of law might well have decided otherwise, but as far as the camp was concerned it was proof enough who the culprit was.

Priscilla was never heard of again. I like to think that she overcame her gregarious nature sufficiently not to find herself once more on the end of a chain. And, if not, that she now and then inflicted a half-Nelson or knee-lock or crushing head-hold on her captor—just for old time's sake.

Illusion and Reality

CAFÉS AND BARS stretched almost the whole length of the shallow curve of the bay and there were tables and chairs on the hard-trodden sand outside. Close to the tables a concrete strip ran parallel with the buildings between the tub-planted rows of palms, and beyond that there were more tables and chairs under a framework of creeper-covered trellis. Beyond that again there was only the sand, silvery green in the moonlight, and the fishing boats drawn up clear of the creaming fringe of water.

The wash of the sea merged with the accordion music drifting out from some of the café radios. It was late, but people still sat at the tables or walked slowly along the concrete strip. Those who walked threw a double shadow: one from the moon, another—more intense—from the acetylene lamps hung on the trellis. Most of the buildings had electric lights above the doors. The lights were dull and yellow in contrast with the moon and acetylene, yet scores of brown moths clung to the colour-washed stone around each one like embossed arrow-heads. The night was sultry, but a silky slide of air persisted off the sea. Now and then there was laughter from the people who went by or lingered at the tables, and it broke the rhythm of the accordion music.

The blind man sat alone beneath the trellis. He was old,

grey-haired, and his back was towards me. He was wearing dark glasses. Outside the café where we sat he and I were the only two under the trellis. One or two others were at the tables nearer the building on the other side of the concrete strip. A white-jacketed waiter, a round metal tray under one arm, stood beside the old man and described the women as they came past.

"What is this one like?" the old man asked.

The waiter shifted his feet. "Beautiful, m'sieur," he said. "Truly very beautiful. Without doubt the most beautiful girl to pass here tonight."

The man wriggled further into his cane chair and nodded satisfaction. The woman going by was very plain, with a body like a barrel. In the queer light her dyed hair was the colour of verdigris and she walked awkwardly, with quick steps, as if in pursuit of her centre of gravity. I put her at forty-five, and that was being charitable.

"A jewel," the waiter went on. "Good long legs, a fine carriage. Red hair, large green eyes; the complexion of a peach." The woman lumped heavily along the strip. "Not more than thirty, m'sieur. Intelligent, too. Intelligence is written all over her face, yet she combines it with charm and vivacity." He paused. "No one more attractive has passed all week. Certainly I have never seen her come this way before."

The blind man grunted, following the sound of the woman's shoes with his head. "Red hair, you say?"

"That is so." The waiter shifted his feet again, a little impatiently. "You will be going now, m'sieur? It is after midnight."

"Soon," the man said. "Soon. I will wait for one more."

The accordion music jolted to an end. The faint hiss of the acetylene lamps seemed to swell, echoing the gritty wash of the sea. From somewhere along the trellis there was a clink of glass; a cascade of laughter. Then the music came again, tango rhythm, ebbing and flowing through the almost imperceptible drift of sea air.

An old couple strolled by, arm in arm. A gendarme, off-duty, trailing a blue-grey swirl of cigarette smoke. Half a dozen young men, students perhaps, coats thrown over shoulders. Then two girls, walking slowly together, glancing from side to side at the people at the tables; peroxide-blonde and short-cut auburn.

The blind man heard the clack of their heels on the concrete. "And these? There are two, yes?"

"Two, m'sieur. Both young. They are against the light, but I will see them better in a moment." He barely looked at them. "They are of even height, dressed in the same style. Very possibly sisters."

Hardly sisters, I thought—unless an overload of rouge and a tired stock-in-trade smile proclaims such an affinity. They were young, certainly, but neither was a beauty. Snub-nosed, one, and enticingly plump, the contours of her body pressing through the looseness of a flowered sleeveless dress. The other was taller, slimmer, in tight black satin that reflected the glare of acetylene along the insolent line of her thighs. The light made their faces an ugly pattern of purple and green; exaggerated the false generosity of their lips.

"Almost certainly sisters," the waiter was saying, bending forward slightly and lowering his voice so they would not hear. "Ah, yes . . . They are as I thought—young, and as fresh as flowers. A wonderfully graceful pair, m'sieur, with much dignity."

"What is the colour of their hair?"

"Both are brunettes, m'sieur."

They were passing now. The peroxided one flashed me a routine smile. The old man listened to the clack of their heels, tilting his head. "Are they as attractive as the one who passed earlier?"

The waiter stifled a yawn. "I would not go as far as that, m'sieur. She was one in a thousand. These two are a fine pair, but you might wait a month before another like the redhead came by."

The blind man clucked his tongue. "She was a jewel, eh?"

"Yes, m'sieur. A jewel."

"A red jewel." He chuckled quietly. "A ruby."

91

He savoured the thought for a moment, then abruptly reached for his stick. The scent of cheap perfume wafted in under the creeper-clad trellis, faded and died away. The accordion music came in sad soft snatches.

"I go now," the man said. He fingered a note carefully before handing it to the waiter. "It has been a pleasant evening; a worthwhile evening. My thanks."

The waiter led him to the edge of the strip. "Tomorrow night, m'sieur?"

"Yes; God granting." He lifted the stick in salute and walked away, cautiously but without hesitation, his grey hair gleaming like a silver cap. "Good night."

"Good night, m'sieur. Au revoir."

The waiter stood with the limp note in his hand, watching him go. After a while he lifted his shoulders and sighed, then came across to my table, thrusting the note into his breast pocket. He was a young man, not unhandsome.

"Another drink, m'sieur?"

"Beer," I said, nodding. It was a good beer. "With the same label on the bottle."

He placed the empty glass and bottle on his tray and wiped the condensation rings from the table. "Every night we have the same performance," he said, anticipating my question. "The old man never tires of it."

"Every night?"

"Except Thursday, when I am not here. He does not come then. He did once or twice, but my relief did not describe the girls to his satisfaction." He smiled, showing even white teeth. "It has been this way for more than a year now. An hour each evening."

"You certainly use your imagination," I said. "Don't you ever tell him the truth?"

He straightened up. "Why should I, m'sieur? Why should I spoil his pleasure? It is a sad world for those of us who can see—a little beauty, much ugliness. Why should I disillusion him? . . . It does no harm," he added, as if I had accused him of something, then went away.

I leaned back and blew cigarette smoke into the roof of the trellis, watching it wrap itself around the creeper. The tables were emptying. Some of the radios had been switched off; a light dimmed here and there. The accordion music was only a vibration now, a background pulse to the hiss of the lamps and the wash of the sea.

The waiter returned with the beer, carrying the tray shoulder high on one hand. He set it down with a smooth, professional flourish.

"What time do you close?"

"Any time, m'sieur. It depends on the customer. In the season it is three, four—sometimes five o'clock. But now—in half an hour, perhaps."

"The earlier it is the better you like it, I suppose," I said, thinking that a young man must have good reasons for wishing to get home, but he only shrugged.

We talked sporadically while I drank the beer. A few people walked along the strip. I played the waiter's game on them, idly imagining to myself what I should say to the blind man if he asked me for a description. I found it difficult, though it was easier if I shut my eyes and made it up without the distraction of reality.

The long glass was almost empty when a girl came by on her own. Even under the greenish glare of acetylene she was attractive. Her black hair had the lustre of enamel; her pale face the innocence of a nun's. She wore sandals and jeans and a white blouse. She walked easily, loose-limbed, with a graceful roll of the hips, high, bold breasts jogging gently under the blouse. When she saw the waiter she half smiled, inclining her head in his direction, then went on. She was humming the accordion music.

"What do you make of that one?" I asked the waiter.

He was drumming his fingers softly on the tray. "That one, m'sieur?" It was a polite, reflex question to cover his inattention.

"Yes. I've tried with some of the others, but I'm not much of a hand at it." I glanced up at him. He was still staring after

93

the girl. "Imagine I'm the blind man. What was that one like?"

He took a deep breath. There was a slight pause. Then he said, "That one, m'sieur, is a fraud. She looks like a saint, a beautiful saint, but any man would find her a she-devil. It would not take him long. Her physical attractions are not as God-given as they seem—but that can be forgiven. I should say that she is a liar and a cheat. Above all, I suspect that she is frequently unfaithful." He laughed in an oddly indignant manner. "I suppose you think that I have been hard on her?"

"Possibly. How can I tell? Right or wrong I marvel at your imagination. Though it would never have done for the blind man, would it?"

"I do not talk about her to the blind man, m'sieur. With him I avoid the truth." He gave a slow, expressive shrug, then nodded along the strip. "She is my wife."

A Bull for the Redhead

THE TRUMPETS STOPPED suddenly. A sound like the rustling of dry leaves slithered over the crowd on the steeply banked tiers around the arena, then whispered away to nothing. Ten thousand people were waiting for Rafael Morales; ten thousand people—and a black Miura bull.

The matador stood behind the barrier in his green and silver suit of lights, holding the red serge *muleta* and the sword across his body. The silence seemed to wrap itself around him and he felt the sweat break cold on his neck. Fear wormed its watery way into his stomach.

"Mother of God!" he said under his breath. "Mother of God, let me not give in to it."

He ran his tongue over his lips. He had been afraid before, though not for a long time—and never like this. It had come over him like a sudden fever, inexplicably, taking him unawares. Out of the corners of his eyes he saw Pepe, his servant, staring at him with a puzzled frown and he was conscious of a slight restlessness, a faint murmuring, in the crowd nearby.

Vultures! he thought bitterly.

A spurt of angry pride ran through him. He squared his shoulders and squeezed through the opening in the barrier, then stepped boldly into the ring. The action seemed to release the tension on his wire-taut nerves.

A sound like rustling leaves whispered again around the arena. The bull was on the far side, in the dazzling half-moon of sunlight. Morales did no more than glance at it. He formally saluted the president before moving along the barrier to where the English redhead was sitting. There were many faces, but he saw only hers. He brought his feet together and held his cap towards her on an outstretched arm.

"This is your bull, senorita," he said, by way of dedication. "A fine brave bull." He paused, wanting to say more, but for some reason the words would not come. "It goes for you," he ended abruptly.

The girl smiled, though not with her eyes. After what had happened last night he expected no better. But then, still smiling, she turned her head towards the man beside her and the coldness went out of her expression. Morales noticed the intimacy of the glance she and the American exchanged. The observation gripped him with a sudden cancerous spasm of jealousy. He turned swiftly on his heels, not wishing to see more, and tossed the cap over his shoulder.

Not now, he warned himself fiercely. Do not think about them now.

The bull had moved to the edge of the shade which curved across the ring like the shadow of a giant scimitar. It stood with lowered head, the coloured banderillas sticking at crazy angles from its neck, and even at sixty feet Morales could hear the angry rhythm of its snorted breath. The inexplicable fear began to dribble into his stomach again. All at once, in the confusion of jealousy and weakness, he felt terribly unsure of himself. Only the leaf-rustle of the crowd—swelling at his momentary hesitation—impelled him forward.

Think of the redhead and the American later, his mind insisted. Think only of yourself now and this great cathedral of a bull. Take him calmly, without tricks. And remember that he hooks to the left.

The bull slewed round at his approach and stood waiting, eyeing him suspiciously. It had fought with speed and ferocity in the earlier stages, and Morales had worked it close—

96

dangerously close—with the cape. He had been at ease then. Not at his best, perhaps, but good enough; better than many will ever be. But now, with the real danger beginning, he could not concentrate his thoughts. The redhead and the bull and the American were all mixed up in his mind. And he was afraid.

He shook the *muleta* loose and transferred the sword to his right hand. The bull stood still, its head going a little lower, the murderous horns pointing. Another silence spread over the arena and he felt it enfold him again, like a huge loneliness. He could hear the animal's heavy breath and the brittle creasing of the silver lamé on his suit of lights as he brought the *muleta* in front of his body and halted sideways on to the bull.

"Toro!" he grunted. "Bull! . . . Hey, beauty!" Its bloodshot eyes glared at the *muleta*. "Come!" he jerked. "Come to me, beauty."

The bull came with an explosive rush. He passed it wide of his body with his feet skipping away, which was bad. The crowd did not approve. The bull turned swiftly and came again, and he passed it in the same fashion. Fear had taken hold of his legs and his feet would not keep still. Sweat half blinded him for a second and he blinked it away. The bull charged a third and a fourth time, but he was scared of it hooking and could not bring the horns any closer past his body. As he finished the series of passes the crowd's roar was shrill with criticism.

"Swine!" he shouted at them, but only the bull heard him above the din.

The last pass had pulled it up short. It stood where sun and shadow met, panting, watching him as he moved in to make a fresh challenge. He gritted his teeth and shuffled two paces forward until he was eight feet away, fighting against the terrible weakness that was engulfing him.

"Toro!" he began. "Hey, toro!"

He was trying to think of nothing but the bull and how it would charge and what he must do when it came . . .

"Come, beauty! . . . Black bull, hey!"

. . . Trying not to think of the redhead and the unpleasantness of last night and the American and what he had noticed just now at the dedication . . .

"Come to me, beauty!"

. . . Trying to steel himself to do it well, without faking, with his feet rooted to the ground and the near horn scraping his left thigh as it passed and the ends of the banderillas slap-slap-slapping his chest.

The noise of the crowd dwindled to a murmur, to a leaf-rustle, to absolute quiet. And then, as he waited for the charge, the sound of a woman's laughter broke the silence. It was a faint laugh, hand-stifled, but Morales recognised it and half turned his head, his concentration gone. As he did so he saw the bull coming. His reflexes swung the *muleta* in a desperately improvised pass, but the bull did not follow the cloth cleanly. It was hooking viciously to the left and he made a frenzied effort to twist his body out of the way. But it was too late. Even before he felt the terrible slash of the horn he knew there was no escape, and in the last split second of painlessness he heard the crowd gasp and the same familiar silky voice rising to a shriek . . .

Morales came out of the dream with a convulsive twitch which jerked him on to his elbows. A truck was grinding up the hill outside and the sound seemed to carry the gasp of the crowd into reality. Every muscle was flexed taut and he stared wide-eyed at the wall. Then, gradually—very gradually—the shocked rigidity ebbed out of him and he lay back on the bed, gathering his scattered wits together.

He had been in the ring, he remembered, and the bull was going to take him. Beyond that he could recollect nothing. Just the bull coming in, ignoring the *muleta*, and the great gasp of the crowd. There had been many such dreams and they always ended at the same moment. But, Mother of God! this was a strong one.

He shivered, as if he were cold, and pushed the scene from

his mind. It was bad luck to probe these things, and today he wanted the luck to be good. Even after seven hundred bulls it was still necessary to have the luck running with you—perhaps more than ever.

Slowly his thoughts took a firmer grip on reality. The vivid climax to the dream was dispelled by the memory of what had happened the previous night. It was not pleasant to think about. He had drunk too much, he knew, but so had the red-head. And so had the American. If it had not been for the American everything might have been all right. As it was, things were said which should not have been said, and now, with his anger gone, the drunkenness gone, he regretted them bitterly . . .

There was a knock at the door and his servant came in, carrying the green and silver suit of lights and the accessories—the ruffled shirt, pink stockings, patent leather slippers and the rest.

"Is it time?" Morales asked.

"You have an hour," Pepe said. He glanced at the matador sprawled in his underclothes on the bed. "How is it with you?"

"Well . . . Well enough. Why ask?"

"You are in a sweat. Have you been dreaming again?"

The big car took him to the plaza. He had left it late and they had to hurry. He sat in the back in his colours, thinking about the redhead. It was important to him that she should be there, but he could not bring himself to hope too much. She also would remember what had happened, and what was said, and he could not be sure that she would wish to forget. He had never been sure of anything about her . . .

The crowds were thick near the plaza and the car nosed through with only ten minutes to spare. Pepe handed him his decorated cape and he draped it over his shoulder and round his waist as he made his way to the tunnel where the parade was forming. He went to his position at the head of his *cuadrilla*, who were ready and waiting. The other two matadors

99

were similarly positioned on his right. He knew one of them. Nobody talked very much. The music from the ring was loud and brassy in the tunnel and the air smelt stale.

The trumpets sounded and the heavy doors swung back. They marched in to the music with a bold swagger, three abreast, and the sudden sunlight made them screw their eyes. Morales searched for the girl as they wheeled towards the president's box, but he could not see her. As they halted and bowed, doffing their caps, he searched again. Then, as the parade broke up and he squeezed behind the barrier, he saw her coming down one of the steep gangways. She was looking for her seat and did not glance his way, but he did not care. The day-long uncertainty left him suddenly and he was smiling as he went to his place and accepted his fighting cape from his servant.

The first bull was his. Released from his preoccupation he gave all his thought to it. The trumpet blasts stunned the air and the door from the pens opened on the far side of the ring. There was a sudden hush; a few seconds' tense delay. Then the bull came, big and black and very fast. He watched it carefully as the *peónes* ran it with their capes, noting its peculiarities. When it was time he stepped into the ring and made the preliminary passes. He was confident and worked it close, pivoting slowly, in the manner the crowds had come to expect of him. Later, while the horses were in and the bull was taking the lance, he worked it even closer, bringing the crowds to their feet.

He felt good. It was going to be his day. After this was over everything would be all right again. He could sense it. It was ridiculous to have believed that the redhead might not come . . .

And then, without warning, as if a switch had been thrown, he was suddenly afraid. The *banderilleros* were in the ring, placing the barbed sticks, and he stood at the barrier holding the *muleta* and the sword across his body. His brain seemed to have gone numb, and he could not understand his fear. He stood there woodenly, heavy-footed, while the frilly sticks

100

were being planted. When it was done and the *banderilleros* ran back to the barrier one of them called to him above the burst of music.

"Watch this cathedral, Rafael. Now it hooks to the left."

The trumpets stopped suddenly. A sound like the rustling of dry leaves slithered over the crowd on the steeply banked tiers around the arena, then whispered away to nothing. Ten thousand people were waiting for Rafael Morales; ten thousand people—and a black Miura bull . . .

Summer Storm

FOR AN HOUR or more they had watched the lightning flicker uncertainly among the shifting mountains of grey and creamy-white cloud in the far distance. At first it had been too remote to trouble them, but now, as the clouds pushed up into the sky and began to tower overhead, they knew it was only a short while before they would be forced to move. Rain was already falling beyond the dark, blue-green hills on the other side of the river, and it was no longer possible to hope that the storm was going to work round the valley. In another ten minutes, perhaps less, they'd have to start collecting the things together and take shelter in the car.

The man turned his head and surveyed the untidy remnants of their picnic lunch before glancing at the woman lying beside him. If she had not spoken a moment or two earlier he might have believed she was asleep. Her eyes were closed and she lay on her back, completely relaxed, apparently unaware of the shadows sliding towards them across the long smooth slope of the hill. The first suspicion of a breeze moved over the grass and tugged gently at her skirt, but apart from an instinctive movement of a hand, she did not stir. She lay there, lips slightly parted, facing upwards towards the last of the sun. And the man, without knowing why, suddenly found himself irritated by her composure.

He looked away again in the direction of the river. More than once since they had parked the car he had been aware of a growing sense of restlessness, yet could not account for it. Now, in these last few minutes, the feeling was stronger than ever, but he was as far from understanding the cause as he was when it first took hold of him.

The lightning flickered sharply, nearer this time; but there was still no thunder. The breeze became more insistent, lifting the edge of the table-cloth they had spread on the grass and sending a crumpled paper napkin dancing into the hedgerow behind them. The man reached for his coat and sat up to put it on, staring moodily down into the valley. The rain had reached the farm at the foot of the hill.

His eyes followed the cart-track which curved up the slope between the fields of clover and mustard. Half-way up, a couple of hundred yards away, there was a gate, and he began looking at it again, as he had done a dozen times already, wondering what on earth it was stuck on the far upright.

A glove, perhaps? No; it was too large for that—somewhere about the size of a football or a person's head. A hat more likely—yes, that was probably it; an old hat which someone had found or discarded and hung on the post as he passed by.

As he rose to his feet the man chided himself for not having thought earlier of such an obvious solution. Perhaps, after all, it was this simple thing which had been worrying him subconsciously most of the afternoon—this, and the approaching storm. And yet, brushing the grass from his coat and trousers, he was not aware of any lessening of the feeling of restlessness. It was with him still, mounting steadily, and as the first drops of rain spattered down he knew that for some reason he wanted to get away from the place as quickly as possible.

The woman opened her eyes and propped herself up on plump elbows. "Darling," she said, blinking at the sky as if rain was the last thing she had expected, "We'll have to move."

He nodded and squatted beside the table-cloth. "Don't worry about the remains," he said. "You go to the car. I'll collect everything in a couple of ticks."

She was on her knees now, patting her hair and groping for her bag with the other hand. "Are you sure you can manage?"

"Quite sure," he replied. "Get a move on or you'll be in for a soaking."

The shadow swept up the hill towards and beyond them as he spoke and the sun had gone. It seemed to turn cold suddenly and the woman shivered slightly.

"You're an angel," she said mechanically, flashing a smile, and walked over to the car.

He opened the picnic-basket and began cleaning the plastic cups and plates with a piece of paper before packing them away. The rain was increasing and there was no time to do the job properly. He bundled the cutlery together, dropped an orange and a couple of apples into the basket, and was leaning over the cloth, nearly at full length, to grasp the coffee flask when the lightning flashed again; close, and violently enough for him to hear it crackle. He was not expecting the thunder. When it came, almost before the lightning had ended, it caught him unawares and automatically he threw himself flat, pressing against the ground as if to escape the deafening roar which cracked and pounded in his ears.

A cold prickling sensation crawled along his spine towards the base of his neck. He looked over the short, stumpy grass into the wide valley. The rain was drifting across it like a smoke-screen. The river was no longer visible, nor was the farm at the bottom of the hill. He could see only the cart-track curving up the slope between the fields and, about half-way along it, the gate with the hat on the upright. He was staring at it, gaping, with his body going rigid and his intestines feeling as if they were melting away, when the lightning stabbed twice, in quick succession, and the thunder burst with the ferocity of an artillery barrage.

At that moment he knew where he was and what he was looking at.

It wasn't a gate at all now. It was the Jap road-block on the side road leading out of Mandalay, and the thing on top was the Lieutenant's head which they had put there on a stick after the first attack failed. He had stared at it through his glasses before the second attack went in, and seen the head as clearly as if it had been ten yards away. Seen the eyes, wide open, looking back at him unwaveringly; the trim moustache on the upper lip and the gleam of the sun on hair and teeth—seen it all, and known that the Lieutenant was alive when, half an hour earlier, two Japs had crawled out and dragged the wounded man behind the block. Seen it, and vomited on the spot. And never, however much he tried, been able to forget—so that now, all these years afterwards, the same fear and sickness welled up inside him as mercilessly as ever before. But never so bad as at this moment.

He wiped the rain off his face and scrambled to his feet again. It would be all right when he got back to the car. He'd feel better then, and they could drive on somewhere else; it didn't matter where. The lightning spat suddenly amongst the sagging clouds and the thunder exploded almost directly overhead. He snatched at the basket and went stumbling along the side of the hedgerow with the coffee flask thrust under one arm. It was only fifty yards to where they had parked the car, yet it might have been ten times as far. All the way, through the beat of the rain, he felt that he was being pursued by something indescribably evil.

The woman was sitting in the back seat, combing her hair. "Darling," she said brightly. "You *have* been a time. Did you get wet?"

"A bit," he said. He flung the basket and coffee flask on the seat beside him and slammed the door. He was shivering, and felt sick and cold.

"Have you brought everything?" she asked.

"I think so."

"What about the table-cloth?"

He looked at the stuff on the seat. "I forgot it," he said wearily.

106

She lowered the mirror and pouted. "Oh, darling," she said. "It'll get soaked. Take your mackintosh and run back for it."

The lightning flashed viciously but, inside the car, the thunder sounded more muffled. The windows were steamed up and he couldn't see outside.

"You go for it," he retorted irritably. "Or wait until all this is over. A wetting won't do it any harm."

She was silent for a moment and he knew she was staring at him. He glanced into the driving mirror and their eyes met. Her expression was one of amused amazement. She leaned forward and nestled her head up against his.

"Poor darling," she said gently, in the sort of voice she reserved for animals and small children, "Of course it can wait. But who'd have thought a great big fellow like you would be scared of a little bit of thunder? . . . Why—you're shaking all over!"

Sapper Murphy's Madonna

SQUAT, SEMI-DETACHED, box-like houses stretched in monot-
onous rows along three sides of the allotments. A shallow,
debris-choked stream curved in a wide arc across the remaining side, separating it from the trees and the green, undulating
spaces of the neighbouring golf course. The bomb was lying
under one of the plots nearest to the stream, almost exactly
half-way between the two end houses. From a safety angle it
could scarcely have been better placed—unless, of course, it
had come down somewhere on the other side of the water—
but, nevertheless, every door and window in the houses had
been opened (here and there some were covered with blan-
kets as an extra precaution) giving the buildings a curiously
deserted appearance.

The Lieutenant had not considered it necessary to have the
occupants evacuated—there was nothing within about a
hundred and fifty yards of where the bomb had been
located—though he was thinking of suggesting that the residents of the nearest houses should leave temporarily when he
started to remove the fuse. It was true the thing had been
buried for the best part of seven years (most of the people
who lived in the vicinity confirmed they'd heard something
drop during the autumn of 1944) but, even so, there was no
telling how high explosive might decide to behave. Only when

the fuse had been drawn would the tension come to an end and the life of the inhabitants in that part of the drab suburb return to normal.

There had been heavy rain during the night, a sudden torrential downpour. In the morning a man, coming to the allotments to lift some potatoes for his wife before setting out for the office, had found a ragged, circular depression about five yards in diameter into which had been sucked the greater part of his vegetable plot. Dismay had quickly given place to speculation and, after calling a neighbour to view the damage, he'd reported the matter at the police station on his way to the Underground. By ten o'clock the Lieutenant had arrived with a couple of men in a light truck and, watched discreetly from a hundred windows, examined the spot with a mine-detector. Twenty minutes later the truck had been driven away, leaving a red flag fluttering lazily on a pole amid the low jungle of cabbages, potatoes and broccoli, and a solitary policeman to keep the curious and over-adventurous at a safe distance.

Another truck had come within the hour, a big three-tonner carrying a multitude of equipment, and with it the Lieutenant, a Sergeant and four Sappers. They'd set to work almost at once, with the quiet efficiency of men who knew what they were doing and exactly how the job should be tackled. An onlooker, unaware of the situation, might easily have imagined they'd arrived to deal with something no more dangerous than a broken gas main.

The local residents had no such illusions. All round the allotments, in every part of the deserted-looking, three-sided wall of houses, they waited anxiously, hour after hour, for news that the danger was over. Nightmare memories, as old as the thing that lay buried near the stream, stirred and forced their way back into people's consciousness. It was as impossible to escape them as it was to ignore the present situation. Men and women, endeavouring to concentrate on their daily routine, found themselves constantly wondering what progress had been made in the small, roped-off oasis among the vegetables, and how much longer the ordeal was

110

going to last. Rumours circulated: ("They say it's a big one . . . Ton or more probably," and "I've heard it's a sort they don't know anything about.") Reassurances, eagerly sought after, were passed on, parrot-fashion, without knowledge or understanding: ("The policeman told me it's only a question of taking the fuse out . . . No danger at all, really. These fellows have dealt with dozens of 'em . . .") The whole area had something of the atmosphere of a besieged fortress, and the tension mounted inexorably as the long afternoon dragged by.

It was a little after four o'clock and Sapper Murphy was digging, twelve feet deep. The bomb was somewhere beneath him, and both he and the three others with whom he'd shared the work, two at a time, since mid-day, were operating with increased caution. There couldn't be much further to go now; three or four feet at the outside—provided the thing didn't start to move. If it did they'd probably have to wait until morning before they could get at it properly, for not more than a few hours of daylight were left.

The man working with Murphy pressed his spade up to the shaft into the buttery clay and grunted.

"Not a sausage."

Murphy licked his lips. The air in the narrow pit was dead, the earth clammy. In another ten minutes or so they'd be relieved and would take their turn at hauling the filled baskets to the surface. Half an hour at a time was as much as they could manage at this depth. Stripped to the waist, their bodies dirt-stained and glistening with sweat, they worked silently; nerves taut, hardly saying a word, conserving their energy. It was like digging in a tomb.

The Lieutenant appeared at the top and watched them for a moment.

"Any sign of water?" His voice sounded strangely amplified and metallic.

Murphy looked up, wiping an arm across his forehead. "Not yet, sir."

111

"Good," the Lieutenant said. "Let's hope it keeps that way."

The two men bent over their work again, probing and cutting carefully into the stiff, yellow earth and loading it, in thick slabs, into the waiting baskets. A couple of minutes passed then, suddenly, Murphy felt something grate against the edge of his spade. He withdrew the tool quickly and dropped on one knee, scraping the clay away with his hands. His companion stopped digging.

"Got a touch?"

"Think so," Murphy nodded, pressing deeper. "Felt something, anyhow."

Gradually, cautiously, he scratched at the clay until, six inches down, his trembling fingers touched the thing again. Disappointment was immediate; it wasn't the bomb— probably nothing more than a stone, and not a very large one at that. He shot a glance at the other man and shook his head, then got to his feet and drove the spade under the point where the object was lying. Once again he felt it jar on the metal. As he brought it up he noticed that what he had at first thought to be a stone was broken in two. A slim, cylindrical stump still protruded from the ground and, even as he reached down and pulled it out, he realised it wasn't a stone after all.

The Sergeant called to him from the rim of the shaft. "Found some potatoes, Murphy, or is it a lump o' gold?"

Murphy grinned. "Not this time, Sergeant. Better than either, maybe."

He had wiped the clay away now and could see the thing more clearly. One glance told him what it was and, with an exclamation of delight, he rummaged amongst the soil for the piece he had first lifted.

The man with him leaned on his spade. "What is it?" he asked.

"A little statue," Murphy said excitedly. "Look!" He held the two pieces together. "It's a Madonna . . . a statue of the Madonna."

"Blimey!" the Sergeant said. "What a thing to find."

The other man spat and returned to his digging without saying a word. Oblivious to his surroundings Murphy continued to stare at the clay-encrusted pieces of terracotta. Then, placing them carefully against the wall of the pit, he picked up his spade. For a moment, just for a moment, he had forgotten he was within a few feet of an unexploded bomb.

The two of them were relieved a few minutes later. It was nearly a quarter to five and the Sergeant went down to do some probing. Murphy stood on the edge of the hole, the air cool on his body, breathing deeply. The sun had reached the tops of the trees on the golf course and long shadows were beginning to stretch across the silent allotments.

He slipped into a shirt, not bothering to tuck it into his trousers, and went over to the Lieutenant. "Permission to break off, sir?"

"Righty-ho," the Lieutenant said. "Ten minutes. And if you're going to smoke get well away from the area." He noticed the statuette under Murphy's arm. "What on earth have you got there?"

"A Madonna, sir." He offered it proudly for inspection. "Just dug it up."

The officer spared it a preoccupied look, and laughed. "Good for you. If you ever dig up a blonde, let me know at once." He glanced anxiously at his watch, and nodded. "Righty-ho, then. Be back in ten minutes."

Murphy followed the path beside the stream until he was a safe distance from the roped-off enclosure where the others were still working, then squatted down and began washing the fractured statuette. The clay gradually disappeared, leaving the pieces clean and fresh-looking. Apart from the break, which ran diagonally across the centre, there appeared to be no other damage.

He lit a cigarette and clambered on to a rubbish heap a little way up from the stream. Sitting there, examining the Madonna, he was like a child with a new toy. It would be easy to mend, he decided, and he would give it to his wife when he went home on leave. She would be delighted with it. They hadn't got such a thing in the house, though they'd often talked about buying one. This would have cost a good deal of money, he reasoned, for it must be very old. And then he began wondering just how old it was, and how it came to be there, buried in the clay under the vegetables.

The bomb exploded just as Murphy decided he ought to be getting back. He never really knew what happened. For a fraction of a second the ground seemed to tremble slightly beneath him. Then, as the blast hit him and the roar of the detonation burst in his ears, the earth gave a great convulsive twitch and he was thrown down the slope of the rubbish dump along with a sudden clattering avalanche of tins and leaves and dead wood.

Ten yards away, at the bottom of the heap, he came to rest. Struggling wildly to his knees, dazed and incapable of hearing anything except the mad scream of a single, continuous note in his ears, he was in time to see the pall of smoke, still compact, hanging in the clear sky like a giant black cauliflower. And he knelt there amongst the rubbish, numbed and bewildered, staring crazily upwards, his fingers still gripping the broken statuette, one piece clutched tightly in either hand.

Twenty-minute Break

WHEN HE WAS first transferred to an outside working-party he had stared at the people passing in the lane, envying them their freedom. He was not alone in that. Each man there, looking across the shallow trough of the valley towards the fringes of life outside the prison walls, experienced the same emotion. With some the envy went deeper, corroding into bitterness and hate, but he was spared that disaster. The effect on him was more subtle; for a long while not fully understood.

Several weeks earlier the girl had passed within a few yards of where he was working. When he'd heard her coming down the lane he'd straightened himself to look at her, anxious that she might greet him in some way; with a nod, perhaps, or a smile. It was only as she walked past, without a sign, that he realised she was blind.

He had seen her often enough, before and since, though always from a distance; and, but for that one brief glimpse of her face at close quarters, he would never have believed she was in any way handicapped. She moved confidently, at a good walking pace, without hesitation. Day after day he had stopped what he was doing to watch her come and go between the prison gates and the square grey house by the bridge. And as he watched, an idea, born out of the vague, confused longing that had troubled him for months past, began to crystallise slowly in his mind.

115

At first he tried to dismiss it, but he could never free himself of it for long. The idea re-awakened whenever he saw her. After a while it got so that he would lie in his cell at night, thinking about her, imagining what it would be like to have her in his arms. "She's blind," a part of his mind argued feverishly. "Blind and lonely. So long as I don't frighten her it will be all right . . . She'll be pleased." As time passed his desire grew slowly into an obsession until he could find nothing to stem the drift of his thoughts. "It'll be all right. Provided she doesn't know where I'm from it'll be all right. She won't mind. She's a sort of prisoner herself, all bottled-up inside—probably never been offered the chance. I reckon she'll be pleased . . . flattered."

Once he had gone that far towards convincing himself, the thought of the penalties that would inevitably ensue no longer served as a restraint. Another part of his mind took over, calculating how he could best make the break . . .

Spring came hesitantly to the valley, softening its bleak expanses with ragged carpets of green and small patches of early fruit blossom. Mist and sagging cloud gave way to thin sunshine and pale, cirrus-strewn skies.

He knew a good deal about the girl now. Some of the old-timers had supplied the information, though he had been careful not to press his questioning too far. She kept house for her father and, from nine till five, while he was on duty at the prison office, she was in the house alone, only leaving it to take him a basket-packed lunch and—occasionally—any mail that came in the afternoon delivery. He also knew that her name was Carmichael; Joan or Jean Carmichael—the men weren't sure which—and he'd picked up various odd details about her father which might possibly prove useful.

All he wanted now was the opportunity; for the weather to give him the chance he needed. But he had left it late. It was unlikely that there would be another of those great rolling seas of mist which had surged so often up the valley during the winter. The best he could hope for was rain—heavy rain, late in the afternoon when the officers in charge of the party were at their least vigilant.

Twice during April conditions were suitable, but on both occasions he hesitated too long. When the moment came he found himself dithering, almost hoping that the rain would cease as quickly as it had begun or that one of the officers would move nearer to where he was working, making it impossible for him to slip away unobserved. Each time his mind seemed to freeze into a state of indecision, and, as his body tensed and the blood pumped suddenly in his throat, he tried to force himself to act, knowing that the slightest move would be irrevocable. In those minutes of crisis he had no thought for the reason which precipitated them. That was something he had come to accept, as essential to his survival as fresh air to a suffocating man.

But, when the chance had gone, the first sensation of relief that he had not committed himself was immediately followed by anger at his vacillation. And the knowledge that he must wait—it might be weeks—for another opportunity only added to his frustration.

During the first week in May it happened. After the mid-day meal they marched to the edge of the woods that straddled the top of the ridge overlooking the prison. The wind had changed direction since morning and the sky was full of tightly-packed cloud, grey and ominous. Because of the nature of the work—they were trimming hedgerows and clearing ditches—the party was more spread out than usual, and the officers had difficulty in keeping the men together. After about an hour he saw the girl going down the lane towards the house and, as he stared at her small figure in the distance, he noticed that rain was falling further along the valley.

A vacuum seemed to form in the pit of his stomach and he felt his pulse quicken. He edged cautiously towards the end of the ditch in which he was working until he was out of sight of the nearer of the two officers. After a couple of minutes he

117

clambered on to the bank and walked back a short way so that he could be seen. It was clear that he had not been missed. A little later, when the officer was looking his way, he deliberately repeated his move, staying perhaps five minutes behind the screen of tall bushes before re-emerging. Again there was no comment; no order to keep close. As he returned along the bank, studying the hedgerow as if he were dissatisfied with some of his earlier work, he felt the first drops of rain on his face and his heart began to thump.

A moment afterwards the rain burst on them with sudden ferocity, blotting out the valley and restricting visibility to a few yards. His mouth was dry and his legs weak as he jumped into the ditch. There was no point in caution now and he stumbled quickly towards the cover of the bushes. When he reached them he shot a glance over his shoulder; then, taking a deep breath, he started to run.

The rain beat on his face like points of cold steel as he plunged down the long slope towards the river. The blood roared and pounded in his ears; the thudding of his mud-heavy boots on the soft earth seemed to come from a long way off. A quarter of a mile of open country separated him from the trees hugging the river bank, and his only thought was to reach them before the rain eased sufficiently for him to be seen from the ridge. Half-way across he tripped and crashed heavily to the ground, but a moment later he was up again, running as fast as his leaden legs would allow him.

The dark shape of a copse loomed ahead. Another hundred yards. He clenched his teeth and made a last desperate effort to increase his pace, but the response was sluggish and he swayed as he ran. Fifty yards . . . twenty-five . . . ten . . . and he was staggering through the undergrowth beneath the trees. For fully a minute he stood there, doubled-up, sobbing for breath, while the green floor of the copse rocked from side to side and his whole body trembled uncontrollably. Then, as strength began to return to his legs and his vision cleared, he turned and peered anxiously towards the ridge.

There was no sign of movement. He could just make out the blurred scar of the woods along the skyline. It was too indistinct to see anything in detail, but the gently-sloping ground in between was deserted. The wind had dropped and the rain fell sullenly from a low grey roof of cloud. For a moment or two he listened for the shrill sound of a whistle, but he could hear nothing through the buzzing in his ears. So far, so good, he thought. He began to thread his way through the trees in the direction of the lane, urged on by the knowledge that, unless the rain soon slackened, the working party would be fallen in preparatory to marching back to the prison. If that happened he would be missed at once.

When he reached the edge of the copse he broke into a trot, keeping the trees between him and the ridge. He could see the outline of the stone bridge now, and beyond it, gradually taking shape, the square box of the house where the girl lived. Almost immediately afterwards he picked out the line of hedgerows that flanked the lane, and he sprinted towards it across an open stretch of field. As he pushed through the bushes on to the road he heard a car coming and he flung himself down, pressing flat against the ground until it had splashed past.

There was no time to be lost, but he paused just long enough to glance behind him, straining his ears for any sound of an alarm. All was quiet, except for the soft hiss of the rain. He scrambled under the hedge and, keeping in to the side of the road, ran at full pelt to the hump-backed bridge. The house was a short distance beyond the far end, fronted by a small garden. He crossed the bridge, bending low so that he was covered by the stone parapet, and forced himself to walk the last fifty yards.

As he turned through the gate in the centre of the garden fence a momentary feeling of panic seized him. For the last few minutes he had been oblivious to everything except the desire to get this far unobserved; the reason for breaking away almost forgotten in the madness of his flight. But now, with the long-imagined opportunity within his grasp, he hesi-

119

tated. The idea which had haunted him relentlessly all these weeks seemed to dwindle suddenly; the familiar, carefully-worded phrases, rehearsed a hundred times in the silence of his cell, faded swiftly from his brain as he stood indecisively at the gate.

Not until he fancied he heard somebody walking down the lane from the prison did he take refuge in action. He hurried along the cement path between the flower-beds, reached for the knocker and rapped firmly on the green-painted door.

There was only a short delay, but every second dragged. He stood to one side of the porch, caught in a fever of anxiety, watching the road and trying to clear his brain in preparation for what was to come. He was on the point of knocking again when, without warning, the door opened and the girl was staring towards him, unseeing, from a yard away.

"Yes?"

He tried to speak naturally, but his throat muscles seemed to contract and no sound came. He could feel the sweat start from the palms of his hands, and a cold emptiness flooded into his mind.

"Yes?" she asked a second time. "Who is it?"

He swallowed hard. "Does Mr. Carmichael live here?" His tongue seemed to get in the way of the words.

"Yes," she said, nodding and opening the door a little wider. "But he's not here at the moment. Who wants him?"

He was prepared for that, answering with the memorised patter about having learned in the village of an old acquaintance being near at hand. "I thought I'd walk over to see him—on the off-chance, you know—before I drove on."

He wished his voice were steadier, more casual. All the time he was speaking he felt certain someone would see him from the road. "Let me in!" his thoughts pleaded. "For God's sake let me in!"

"Well, I'm afraid you're unlucky." It was unnerving the way she seemed to stare at him. "He's up at the prison at the moment and won't be back till just after five."

120

"I wouldn't mind waiting," he said.

"For a couple of hours?" She smiled faintly. "It'd be quicker if you went up to see him at the office. It's only about a quarter of a mile. You can ask for him at the side gate."

His mind was moving towards panic again. His thoughts were chaotic, and he struggled desperately not to let them lead him into pushing his way inside. That would be fatal. He felt certain he could hear footsteps from the direction of the bridge, yet, even as his nervousness mounted, he was also conscious—deep down—of the nearness of the girl, of her smooth bare arms, the curve of her breasts under the yellow blouse, her brown, loose-curled hair . . .

"It's raining," he said, barely concealing his frantic anxiety. "It's only come on since I parked the car, and—"

"Raining?" She took a step forward and held out a hand, palm upwards. "Why, so it is. Look, I'm sorry. Come in for a moment, will you?"

He followed her in quickly, relief surging and tingling through him in a great flood so that, momentarily, he forgot the significance of his entry.

"You must think I'm very rude, making you stand there in the rain," the girl went on. "Have you got an umbrella?"

"No." He was afraid she would offer him one. "If you don't mind I'll wait until it lessens . . . It won't last long. Then I'll go up to the prison."

"All right," she said, shutting the door by leaning against it. "What a pity you left your car in the village. Are you very wet?"

"No, not very. I'll soon dry out."

Automatically he looked down at his mud-caked boots and baggy stained uniform, and it was only then, for the first time, that he really understood the enormity of what he had done—and of what he had come to do. The realisation caught him off his guard and he felt suddenly scared.

"There's a fire in the kitchen," the girl was saying.

He stood clumsily aside for her to pass and let her show him into a small, over-crowded room, where there was a

121

cooking-range set in a recess. She moved between the furniture with the same assurance that he had noticed when she was in the lane. Everything about her was quick and confident.

"There," she said brightly. "How's that?"

"Fine," he heard himself reply.

"Put the radio on if you want. It's over there." She pointed. "I'll make some tea. You could do with some tea, couldn't you? The kettle's almost on the boil."

"Thank you, yes."

She pottered about, her hands finding what she wanted with almost uncanny accuracy. He stood with his back to the fire, watching her, seeing her thickish legs, the wide, unrouged lips and the whiteness of her skin just above the neck of the blouse, and part of his mind was thinking, "You haven't got much time. You can't just stand here, letting the minutes go by. You've got to hurry."

"Did you know Father during the war, in the army?"

"That's right," he lied, grateful that she should make it easier for him.

She seemed to hesitate. "You're not Mr. Hudson by any chance?"

"No. My name's Roberts," he lied again.

"Ah." She brought the spout of the kettle into contact with the tea-pot before starting to pour the boiling water. "Father's often talked about a Mr. Hudson, and I just wondered."

Through the window he could see the rain still falling in a greyish drizzle against the background of hawthorns in the garden. His thoughts started nagging at him again, but he found himself incapable of acting as they demanded. The scared feeling was still with him, distracting him, and with it there was a half-recognised sense of shame, a sort of emptiness, that had come with the sight of his uniform, wet and muddy after the flight, and the realisation of what he had done and why he had done it.

The girl went on talking as she set the tea-pot on the table

122

and felt her way to the dresser for cups and saucers. Now and then he spoke too, and though he kept an instinctive guard on his tongue his head was throbbing with the uncertainty of what was going on outside, thinking of the working-party and the rain and what would happen when he was missed . . . wondering whether he'd been missed already.

"D'you like sugar, Mr. Roberts?"

It was almost two years since he had been asked that question. The abrupt, kindly way in which she spoke seemed to reach deep into him, pushing through the layers of self-pity and wretchedness that had accumulated since he was sentenced, and—without knowing why—he found himself strangely moved, as if his pride had been stirred.

"No, thanks," he said.

She turned towards him, and again he had the queer feeling that she could see. "Sure? We've plenty."

"No, thanks," he repeated. "I never take it."

As she lifted the tea-pot the spout caught the top of the jug of milk, knocking it sideways. The milk splashed across the blue and yellow check cloth and plunged over the edge of the table in a swift white cataract.

She gave a little suppressed cry. "Is that the milk?"

"Yes." He was at the table, quickly, righting the jug. "Some of it's saved, though."

"That's the second time today," she sighed exasperatedly. "Is it very bad?" Her hands began to explore the cloth, discovering the extent of the damage, and he noticed that they were shaking.

"No. Might be worse." A thin column of milk still dribbled to the floor, where it spread in a pool on the worn linoleum. "Is there anything to mop it up with?"

"I'll do it—" she began.

"No. Tell me where to look."

It was not until he was on his knees by the table with a milk-soaked rag splodging between his fingers that he realised exactly what he was doing. Everything had happened at such speed that he'd acted on impulse, yet now, although the

123

girl's legs were close to his head as he swabbed with the rag he was scarcely conscious of them. The desire that had consumed him for so long had evaporated; the scared feeling gone. Instead, he found himself suddenly overcome by pity for her, and, almost as if the situation were a cue for something he had learned by heart, he remembered how, in his cell, he'd argued his case with "She's a sort of prisoner herself, all bottled-up inside." As he got to his feet the phrase drummed in his brain, and he knew what a terrible understatement it was. Despite her apparent certainty and confidence he could sense the nervous tension, the strain, the constant longing that fretted beneath the surface—and would continue to do so, not for three years, or ten, but always . . .

"Shall I put the rag where I found it?"

"Please." She laughed a little awkwardly. "Fine one I am to make a caller do all the work."

She placed a couple of small cork mats under the stained area of the cloth, then began to pour the tea again. "Second time lucky," she said as she handed him his cup. "Father's always worried about me being here alone during the day. Says I'll burn the house down or something."

"You manage very well."

"You're being polite," she said. "Fancy saying that—after the mess I've just made!"

They talked together more easily now. For two or three minutes he forgot about the time and the rain and the working-party up on the ridge. In that brief period, as the tea warmed him and he enjoyed the unaccustomed comfort of a leather-padded armchair, as the surroundings of the small, crowded room revived old memories, he began to understand that, above all, it was this he had longed for subconsciously during the last few months—the restoration of his shattered self-respect. When she had passed him in the lane several weeks ago he had not known why he had wanted her to acknowledge him. But he knew now, and because of his pity for her he had learned something more besides—a measure of humility.

124

The clock on the shelf above the cooking-range ting-ed softly. Quarter past three. He stared at it for a moment, surprised to find there was no sudden reaction of panic as the truth dawned on him, only a strong sensation of disappointment that the minutes had gone so rapidly.

"How's the rain?" the girl asked.

He looked out of the window. "Stopped," he said. He hesitated for a moment, then, "I'd best be going."

"Won't you have another cup?" She sounded as if she really wished he would stay.

"No, thanks. Really, I'd better push off."

He followed her into the hall and let her open the door. The lane was empty.

"Turn left," she said. "The prison's straight on—a quarter of a mile. You can't miss it. Ask at the side gate—they won't let you in otherwise."

"Thanks," he answered. "And thanks again for the tea."

"You're welcome."

She was still standing at the door when he reached the gate. As he stepped into the deserted lane and turned in the direction of the prison he was aware of an almost overwhelming sense of freedom, as if a great burden had been lifted from his mind. At the hump-backed bridge he had his first view of the woods along the skyline and he could see the working-party, a tiny ant-like phalanx, being marched across the open slope of the ridge. One of the officers was running on ahead and, very faintly, the high-pitched note of a whistle, repeated over and over again, pricked the still silence of the cool rain-washed air.

He watched the scene with a curious feeling of detachment. The vivid sense of freedom was still with him as he walked steadily down the lane towards the prison gates. It had become part of a tremendous elation, an elation he had never before experienced. No matter what they might do to him, he knew that the past twenty minutes had been splendidly worthwhile.

125

Self-portrait

THE FULL STORY of William Jefferson Scott is altogether another matter. This is about one of his paintings—the self-portrait he did not long before the madness finally swamped his brain and destroyed him.

Technically, it has its faults. But, physically and mentally, it lays him bare with a frankness so remarkable that you almost recoil from your first sight of it. Unless you are absolutely blind you can hardly fail to understand why his short life went the tragic way it did.

Liam Scott—that's how he always signed himself—was a savage; a shambling, uncouth giant of such monstrous ugliness that no woman would come near him, not even to sit for him. This has been said of other men, not always truthfully. But—God knows—it is true of Scott. And—God knows—a woman was what he wanted more than anything in this world.

Every detail of his ugliness is in the picture. But it is the stark portrayal of his frustration—the animal longing in the eyes, the pent-up passion in the curve of the thick lips—which makes you blink and look again. All in all it is one of the most brutal self-revelations I have ever known. Over and above the massive force of the gorilla-like figure, the impression it gives is of an overwhelming sense of despair; a bitter, bestial yearning, which, coupled with the physical ugliness, never fails to send an odd shiver along my spine.

The first time I saw the picture was just before the war at one of the galleries. A Liam Scott never fetched a great deal, but in those days almost any price was beyond my pocket. In any case it had been sold when I got there.

The war was on when Scott hanged himself. I hadn't forgotten the picture, but the news re-awakened my interest in it. I was curious to know its whereabouts and when I eventually returned home I made enquiries. But the gallery and its records had been destroyed by an incendiary, and the manager couldn't recall to whom the sale had been made. So I gave up trying to find out.

Then, quite by chance, I came across the picture in an auction-room. It was stacked behind some furniture with three or four others—they weren't his—and the catalogue confirmed that they were all coming up in one lot. Time had not made me any less receptive to its tremendous power and I was determined to have it. The whole tragedy of William Jefferson Scott's life was on that canvas, just as surely as if someone had written a book about him.

It came up for sale the following day. I had expected the competition to be pretty fierce, but there were only three others interested in it and two of them dropped out quite early on. I was near the back of the room, so as to keep a better eye on the opposition, yet I couldn't discover who the last of the trio was. It could have been any of a group of heads up front on the left. The auctioneer sang out the price, looked at me, accepted my nod, tapped the air impatiently with his hammer and offered the new figure to the assembly. Then, taking his silent cue from somewhere in front, he raised the price again and glanced eagerly in my direction. The same routine must have been repeated a dozen times. But at last, at forty pounds, there was some hesitation on the part of the other bidder.

"Guineas?" the auctioneer suggested. There was a pause. He waggled the hammer. "Forty guineas?" He widened his field, surveying the room. "Forty pounds I'm bid. Who'll make it guineas?" Another pause. "No? . . . Right then. Forty pounds it is." And the hammer came down with a crash.

It had not been my intention to go so high, but I had made up my mind not to lose the portrait a second time. I went round to the back to see what could be done about re-offering the other three pictures, which I didn't want. At the clerk's desk there were a number of people ahead of me, so I walked over to where Lot 87 had been placed against a wall. The Liam Scott was behind the others and I drew it out and stood it in front of them. It affected me with all its old force, and the combination of ugliness and imprisoned desire in the twisted face and gorilla body sent the same odd shiver along my spine.

Then a girl's voice said. "Excuse me. But was it you who bought Lot 87?"

She couldn't have been more than twenty-two or three. Her hair was fair and she was very pretty.

"Yes," I said.

She hesitated. "This is a stupid question, I suppose, but you wouldn't by any chance change your mind? Or partly change it?"

"How d'you mean?"

"Well, I was wondering if you really wanted all four pictures."

She smiled, an honest, simple sort of smile that had no guile in it, and it made her look even younger and prettier. She had the innocence of face of a Dresden china shepherdess.

"As a matter of fact I don't."

"Which ones are you keeping?"

"Only the portrait."

"The Scott? D'you really want the Liam Scott?"

"Indeed I do." I smiled. "Don't tell me that's what you're after."

"I bid for it," she said.

"*You?*" I gazed at her in astonishment. "What do you know about Scott?"

"Know about him?" The long, fair lashes fluttered. "Nothing . . . Should I know something? I like his picture, that's all. Isn't that why one buys a picture?"

I stared unbelievingly at the delicate peaches-and-cream face. "Why do you like it?"

She looked away from me, at the portrait. And deep in her eyes and in the unconscious curl of her lips I saw something which shook me. It was as if I were peering through a key-hole into the private recesses of her mind, and I felt suddenly embarrassed.

"Why?" the girl was saying. "I . . . I don't quite know why."

But I did. And now, whenever I glance at the portrait, two faces look out at me; two faces with an identical expression—an expression which never fails to send an uncomfortable shiver along my spine.

What Goes Up
Must Come Down

KILLING IS NOT—perhaps I should say *was* not—my line. For nine years or more I've lived quietly in a boarding house just off the Bayswater Road and, I like to believe, given offence to no one. Five and a half days at the office in the City, weekends with either my brother or sister, an occasional theatre in the evening or, perhaps, a couple of hours at my Club—that, in a few words, has been the routine since the war ended. And now—murder.

It seems impossible, but it's true: and, what is more, I believe I've got away with it.

Hate is a terrible, devilish emotion, and until I returned from Germany in 1946 it was mercifully a stranger to me. But when I got home that damp, early-autumn afternoon and found that Soames and my wife had been having an affair, it was born. Only now—since last Thursday to be exact—has it left me, and fear taken its place.

I have no wish to recount the details of those terrible weeks at the end of 1946. They are too painful for me to dwell upon at any length. I will merely record that Soames took my wife from me and then, when he had tired of her, abandoned her for somebody else. In little more than two years he had reduced her from a healthy young woman to a neurotic slut, and she committed suicide within a month of his leaving her.

131

Soames killed her as surely as I killed him, though—by his death—he has escaped the nagging anxiety which has enveloped me since last Thursday, when I met him in the Battersea Park Pleasure Gardens.

It happened quite unexpectedly. I had gone along that evening on a sudden impulse, telling myself that, if I were ever going at all, it would be better to do so before the summer was over. Subsequent events have rather confused my memory about all I did while I was there, but, on the whole, I should say I enjoyed myself. I'm middle-aged now, and somewhat reserved—which comes of living so much on my own—but, once in the Fun Fair, I found the carnival atmosphere infectious and I tried my hand at pretty nearly everything—from the Big Dipper to the coconut-shies. It cost me a pound or two, but it was worth it, and by the time I came to leave I had a bread-knife as a souvenir of my skill on the pin-tables.

There were still a number of people about as I made my way to one of the exits, and the noise and hurdy-gurdy music were as loud as ever. I edged through a narrow opening between two of the stalls and cut across the grass behind some piles of straw and empty packing cases. Except for one other person walking towards me, I was suddenly alone. My eyes were unaccustomed to the gathering dusk after the glare of the lights and the other person was almost level with me before I saw him clearly.

It was Soames. Nine years since I last met him—yet, in that moment of recognition, all the old hatred flared up, engulfing me in its intensity. I have lived it again a hundred times, at all hours of the day and night, and have a vivid, nightmare recollection of the sudden explosive force of my rage. But of the act itself I remember nothing. The next thing I can recall with any certainty is standing over his body and seeing the bread-knife quivering in his throat. Then I was running . . . running, and I didn't stop until I had joined the stream of homeward-bound people crowding the main exit. Somewhere on the way back to my room I was sick . . .

The papers carried the story in the morning—no doubt you

132

read it. I went to the office that day and tried to concentrate on my work. Over the weekend I nearly drove myself mad with worry. But, by the time the police called to see me a couple of days ago, I had calmed down sufficiently to be able to answer their questions satisfactorily.

They had got in touch with me, they explained, because they understood the dead man had been named as the co-respondent in my divorce. Amongst other things, they were anxious to know when I had last seen him and whether I could account for my movements on the night he was killed.

I told them I had not seen Soames since 1946, and that my landlady would confirm I had spent the evening in my room. There were a dozen or more additional questions and I was thanked for my co-operation. Since then they have left me alone. As I said earlier, I think I've got away with it.

Why? Because the landlady saw me come in on my return from the office that particular evening, but she neither saw me go out again nor come back the second time. If she had the game would be up, here and now; but I know she believes I never left the house. There's nothing much else for the police to go on. Scores of identical bread-knives must be won by people every night. My finger-prints were not on the handle because I had put on my gloves when the knife was given to me just before I decided to come away. I'm quite safe on that score.

One thing worries me though—almost to distraction. During the course of the evening I entered for one of those long-distance balloon races. Mine was a yellow balloon, I remember, and the last I saw of it it was climbing fast over the trees towards the north-west with the tie-on label waggling underneath like a stiff white tail. Anyone finding the balloon is asked to return the label to the organisers. If that happens the police will be on to me like a shot. Quite literally my alibi will have gone sky-high and I won't have a snowball's chance in hell.

Why? Because the label carried my name, address *and the date*.

Girl Friday

EVERY FRIDAY, RAIN or shine, she used to arrive at my office to clean the telephone, smartly dressed in a green serge uniform and looking as pretty as a picture.

Sharp on ten o'clock I would hear her walking briskly down the corridor towards my room and a moment later she'd be inside, smiling all over her face as if she was really pleased to see me. Five minutes afterwards, her work done, she'd shut the little fibre case she always carried, finish whatever it was she was telling me and make for the door. A parting wink— and she was gone. It was the same every Friday and, although it would be an exaggeration to say that I looked forward to seeing her, her brief visits became one of the more pleasant interludes in the week's routine.

It must be nearly two years now since she started coming. She was small, pert and talkative, with a mass of curly dark hair, large hazel eyes and a Cupid's bow of a mouth. She was pretty all right, and to have worn that uniform as well as she did showed there wasn't much wrong with her figure either. But, above all, she was talkative.

As the weeks went by and the number of five-minute visits mounted, I began to find that I knew a good deal about her—how much she earned, where she lived, how her husband was employed, what they did with themselves in the evenings, and much more besides. Bit by bit, as the weeks became months, my knowledge of her private life increased with each short session, and I was informed of her views on the Korean business, the latest T.V. programmes, President Truman, the cost of living—and a dozen and one other things. She was never at a loss for a subject and, while it would probably have been tedious to spend more than a few hours continuously in her company, for five minutes at a stretch I found her stimulating and unfailingly cheerful. And I always made a point of stopping whatever I was doing when she arrived so that I could listen to each fresh instalment without being distracted.

At first she used to devote a good deal of time to descriptions of her husband and his activities. He was an insurance salesman ("Five years older than me—he's just turned twenty-seven") and they'd only been married a short while. His work involved an occasional trip away from home and when that happened she was either a bit down in the mouth about it, or, depending upon his time-table, full of expectancy about his return. It was, I suppose, only natural that her references to him should have become less frequent as the months passed by, and I attached no significance to it when other and more varied matters gradually crept into our conversation. Anyhow, it was nothing to do with me, and she continued to be as perky as she was punctual.

I used to tease her sometimes and she took it very well. One day she said, "Went out dancing last night. Swell band. Reckon I must have covered about twenty miles. That's what it seems like this morning, anyhow."

"Tired?"

"I'll say," she yawned. "Worn out."

"I thought you always went to the movies on Thursdays?"

"So we do usually, but it makes a change."

"Don't tell me your husband's a dancer too."

She was spraying the mouthpiece with disinfectant. "He's away until Saturday. I went out with a girl friend."

"I'd stick to that story if I were you," I grinned and, to my surprise, she blushed.

"It's true," she said, somewhat indignantly. "Joan White. Works in the chemist's near where I live."

"I remember," I said. "You told me about her. Engaged to a boy in the Marines. Isn't that the one?"

"You're smart, you are," she retorted approvingly.

She started packing her case and was silent for a moment or two. Then, hesitantly, she said: "As a matter of fact, I *did* meet somebody at the dance. Comes from Pittsburgh— Sergeant, I think he is. Wants to see me again."

"I'm not surprised."

"He was nice. Danced well and was very good company— you know what I mean?"

"I can guess," I said. "When does he want to see you again?"

"Tonight. Suggested we had a few drinks and went to the movies."

I didn't like the sound of it and told her so. "What about your husband?" I added. He was just a name to me, but I'd heard enough about him in the past to make me feel he wasn't a complete stranger.

"He won't know," she said easily. "And even if he did he can't expect me to sit around doing nothing whenever he's away. It's not natural, is it?"

She paused in the doorway waiting for me to say something; a word of encouragement perhaps, but I hadn't one to give. I shrugged my shoulders. "It's your funeral, not mine."

"You *are* gloomy today," she replied cheerfully, and flashed a farewell smile. "Well . . . so long. Don't do anything I wouldn't do."

For the next couple of weeks she talked of nothing except the soldier. She was seeing him regularly, without her husband's knowledge, every three or four days. It seemed that he was stationed close by and was able to get in to meet her fairly frequently. When she called on the last Friday in August I told her she was being stupid and that it would only lead to trouble; but she just laughed and said she wouldn't have thought I was so old-fashioned.

Someone else came the following Friday. A tall, synthetic blonde with far too much make-up and a nasty rumbling cough. I was so surprised that I just stared at her for a moment without speaking. She was round at my side of the desk and had opened her case before I said anything.

"What's happened to . . . to the regular girl?"

"I wouldn't know," the blonde one coughed. "Hasn't been in for a couple of days. I'm doing relief."

"I see," I said, and was left to wonder.

But not for long. Next morning I saw the headlines in the papers—GIRL FOUND STRANGLED IN BEDROOM—and there was a picture of her, spread across two columns, underneath. They were making a big story of it, but except for the details about the manner of her death there wasn't anything I didn't already know. It was all there, both about her and her husband. And in the stop-press there were half a dozen lines reporting that he'd been charged with murder.

Another girl comes now; a different girl altogether. She seems quick and efficient, for she's out of my office in no time and the telephone's always left spotlessly clean. She comes every Friday as usual; carries a little fibre case and wears the same green serge uniform. Apart from that I couldn't give you her description, even if I tried. I don't know anything about her, not one single thing, and I intend to keep it that way. It seems to me there's a lot to be said for not knowing too much about people you meet. There's enough trouble as it is.

A Sudden Frenzy

Mrs. Gordon Blake hesitated at the edge of the pedestrian-crossing. The High Street was always at its busiest on early-closing day; the traffic more relentless. Twice she made a hopeful forward move and was twice defeated. A young woman with a pram joined her presently and they waited together. "Worse than trying to get through a revolving-door," the newcomer commented cheerfully and Mrs. Blake agreed.

The day's shopping, never less than an irksome necessity, was increasingly becoming a frustrating and harassing experience. For one thing, the housing estate was far enough out to involve a bus journey and the hourly service was quite inadequate: miss a bus—either way—and her morning's schedule was ruined. All too often that happened and Gordon had to wait for his lunch. And all too often Barnfield's narrow pavements were so crowded that, even when she *did* manage to get back to the bus station in time, she was quite exhausted from all the pushing and queueing—let alone the hazards of making several crossings of a double stream of traffic.

"Sooner they finish that by-pass the better, if you ask me," the woman with the pram announced. "Come on, Canute," she called impatiently to the police constable on the island. "Do something, can't you? We haven't got all day."

The constable feigned deafness and took his time. Eventually he acted and perhaps a score of people hastened from one pavement's edge to the other. The sun was hot and a lorry belched diesel fumes, a combination which gave Mrs. Blake a momentary feeling of nausea. She felt suddenly that she couldn't stand being hemmed in and herded about any longer.

"Damn!" her companion exclaimed. Against her will Mrs. Blake helped free one of the pram's wheels from a drain-grating. The pink and white child in the pram eyed her with slobbering contempt. "It's all right for *you*," the woman said to it in mock-anger. Then, with a sidelong grin: "Doesn't know when she's well off, that's the truth."

Mrs. Blake smiled wanly and went her way, struggling through a purposeful tide of bustling humanity, growing increasingly indignant every time her progress was checked or a thrusting shoulder rammed her off balance. Armitage, the butcher. Then Mence Smith. Then the greengrocer . . . How was it, she thought bitterly, that so many women never seemed to lack time for a leisurely coffee or a quiet gossip? It was Gordon's fault, really. Other husbands quit the house after breakfast and didn't come home again until late afternoon or early evening. But not Gordon. As Park Superintendent he was barely a quarter of a mile from the house at the best of times. "No cafés for me," he always said. "And no flask and sandwiches either. I like a proper mid-day meal, thank you very much." Yes, Mrs. Blake thought with increasing venom, all the tension and discomfiture were really his fault.

She waited her turn at the butcher's, then left with three lamb chops in her basket. Nearly a quarter past eleven. The bus pulled out of the yard on the half hour. Fuse wire from Mence Smith. Apples, potatoes and carrots . . . Irritably, she threaded towards the greengrocers, queued once again, sticky and on edge. She had never much cared for the assistant who eventually attended to her, and on this particular morning his brusque manner struck her as downright offensive.

"Six and nine?" she queried tartly.

140

"Two pounds apples, two and four; pound of carrots, eight-pence; three pounds potatoes, three and nine." Grimy hand cupped, he rattled up the addition. "Six and nine altogether. If you can make it less, missus, I'm a Dutchman . . . Next?"

Dismissed, she paid and walked out, infuriated by the wink directed over her shoulder. The basket was heavy now and dragged at her arm. Fuming, she started towards the Mence Smith shop. Rather than attempt the more direct approach across the Square she committed herself to a side-turning and cut through behind the Town Hall. For fifty yards or so there were fewer people; a welcome absence of cars. But outside the red-brick Police Station a sizeable crowd barred her way. A burly constable was doing his best to restrain it from spreading across the whole width of the narrow street.

"Come on, ladies," he was saying. "Back on to the pavement, if you please. I want this carriageway kept clear. If it isn't I'll move the lot of you on. It's up to you."

Mrs. Blake, attempting to push through the throng, found herself alongside the young woman with the pram. But for this second meeting she would probably have struggled past, too intent on the clock to allow her curiosity any rein. There were barely seven minutes to spare before the bus left and she would only just make it in time.

"They've got him," the woman said, clutching at her arm.

"Got who?"

"The man who did in that boy last night. You know—the poor little kid they found on the building site down Arlington Road way. Only seven, he was."

A memory stirred in Mrs. Blake. There had been something in the morning paper, though she had only glanced at it briefly.

"They say they're bringing the bastard in now," the one with the pram said. "My God, the bastard . . . I know what I'd like to do with him, and that's straight."

The crowd pressed more tightly, squeezing the two of them together. There was hardly a man in it. Hats, head-scarves —Mrs. Blake could scarcely see the entrance to the Police

141

Station. She couldn't have left now even if she had wanted to. On all sides there was the pressure of elbows and shopping-baskets. The sibilant voices around her were charged with a mixture of horror and hatred.

The child in the pram started to bawl. "Shut up, you, for God's sake," the young woman snapped, peering down the street. Three constables emerged from the main door and began trying to clear a path through to the kerb. Mrs. Blake glanced up at the Town Hall clock. She would never get the bus now. Lunch would be late again and Gordon would be on at her as usual. She trembled with suppressed rage, hurt and indignant, her mood tainted by the vindictive disgust and loathing filling her ears.

"Here he comes!"

The crowd swayed. There was some scurrying around its edges. Standing on tip-toe Mrs. Blake glimpsed a black saloon turn into the street. The woman beside her slapped the crying child across the cheek. "Shut *up*, can't you?"

"Back now, ladies. Keep the kerb clear. Come on, now—move . . . That's better."

A sudden quiet descended as the car drew up, a quiet filled by the Town Hall clock striking the half hour. Then, as if a signal had been given, several women simultaneously started to scream obscenities. Mrs. Blake could only just see the top of the car and the upper part of a near-side door as it swung open. Something foul and unfamiliar was beginning to possess her—something which welled up from a tiny and unrecognisable point deep within; uncontrollable, vicious.

"You bloody sod," she heard herself muttering. "You filthy sod."

She saw two men, head and shoulders only, with someone between them, anonymous under a grubby raincoat shroud.

All around her the shouting increased. She added her voice to it, her free hand clenched in rage, face-high. "Oh, you sod! You filthy sod!"

The trio fought its way through to the entrance and disappeared. Only then was Mrs. Blake really conscious of her

142

own voice. As the crowd began to thin she seemed to have the savage echo of what she had shrieked ringing inside her head. Trembling still, but with a growing sense of shame, she made for Mence Smith, somehow purged—though of what she did not know.

The raincoat was removed from the man's head only when he had been led into the Inspector's office. Someone pushed a chair forward and he sat down, blinking against the rush of light.

"Now," the Inspector said quietly from across the wide desk. "Let's begin at the beginning. Your full name is—?"

The man licked his lips before answering. "Gordon John Blake," he said.

Turn and Turn About

WHEN HE FIRST set eyes on her she was billed as *L'Oiseau d'Or* and she was seventy feet above his head at a tented circus near Madrid. Now he called her Tony, short for Antonia, and she knew him simply as Clay—that, and no more. They never went far with names. She was as small-boned and beautiful and daring as a bird, and within seconds of seeing her he had felt for sure that she was the one for him.

"What are you doing with the rest of your life?"—old movies have such lines. Yet these were the words he'd used, and only five weeks ago. Since when the two of them had discovered the seclusion of this rented salt-white villa perched amid the spectacular coastal scenery of Sardinia. "Love me, bird girl?" he would ask and, as often as not, she would wrinkle her nose and frown a bit and pretend to give it serious consideration.

She was, he guessed, in her very early twenties. Her hands were enormously expressive, compensating for occasional lapses in her slightly accented English. Her mother, he learned, was Spanish and her father came from Poland; both were circus people, still active with a juggling routine somewhere in the States. She had Modigliani eyes, brown, wonderfully alert, and her straight raven-dark hair was shoulder length. What her surname was she had never told him, and it didn't matter; Tony was label enough.

"Tony," Clay said now, watching her, "you're gorgeous."

"Thank you."

"More so every day."

"You are a great flatter."

"Flatter*er*," he corrected.

"You're so clever, and I'm a dense."

"Dunce."

"All right, but a dunce in four languages." The line of her lips was tighter than she realised. "At least I am not a prisoner of my tongue, like you and all the other English."

He grimaced amiably. "*Touché.*" Then he kissed her.

"Give me a cigarette, will you?"

Clay lit one and transferred it direct to her mouth. They were by the pool, stretched out on loungers. Olive skin and pink bikini—every time he ran his eyes over her he marvelled. He was thirty years old, stocky and muscular. His hair was short and crinkled, his eyes blue. Only an enemy could have suggested he was anything but handsome. He had told her he was a Londoner, which made straightforward sense, and explained that he was in the metal business—"exclusively non-ferrous"—which didn't interest her enough to question whether it made sense or not.

"How about a drink?"

"Please," she said. "A Cloudy Sky."

"Does that mean gin and ginger beer?"

He got up and began to pad around the pool's edge. "Know something?" he said, turning his head. "You're a gift, bird girl. A pure gift."

He slipped as the last word left his mouth. For a few seconds he was all arms and legs, wildly trying to retain his balance. Finally, like a drunken dancer, he pirouetted on the wet tiles and crashed down.

"Clay! . . . Are you all right?"

For a moment he didn't move. Then he pushed himself into a sitting positon.

"All right?"

He nodded. She began to laugh, head back. But when she looked at him again his face was contorted and he was gripping both ankles.

"Clay—"

"Wow." His eyes widened with pain. "*Wow* . . ."

"What is it?"   She squatted anxiously beside him: "Broken?"

"Shouldn't think so."

"I'll call a doctor."

"Let's get up first."

He struggled on to the nearest lounger and gingerly explored the damage.

"Well?"

"Really turned them over, didn't I?" He sucked in air between clenched teeth. "Left one's not so bad. But the right—ayeeeee . . ."

Her hands fluttered. "Is it bones?"

"Bones, no. Muscles, ligaments."

"Muscles—ah."

She rose at once and went into the house. When she came back she carried an ice bucket and a wad of table napkins. She wrapped crushed ice in a napkin and draped the compress gently round Clay's right ankle.

He said: "You've done this before."

"In a circus these things happen."

"Hardly with my flair and style."

"We are not all with your talent."

"Bitch," he said.

"Now you have to take it easy and look at the view."

"I know all about the view. I've seen it before."

"Only robbers and gipsies say you must never return. Which one of those are you?"

"Of all the bloody things to have happened . . . Tony, girl, you're looking at a prize idiot."

"I know it."

"All done by — ouch! — mirrors. Incredible, isn't it? Nothing up my sleeves."

147

She slid away from him, pushing a cushion under the extended leg. "You need to keep it high."

"Is that so?"

"And tonight, if it isn't any better—"

"Tonight, if it isn't any better, the nurse will be in trouble."

"Tonight," she smiled, "if it isn't any better, your problems will be to catch the nurse."

"I'll manage," Clay said.

"It would not surprise me."

He winced slightly. "You, bird girl, are a great flatter."

Later in the afternoon she drove the Fiat to the village. It was a corkscrew stretch of road, narrow and unpredictable, offering head-on glimpses of the sea one moment and mountain views the next. Figs and olives grew on the bordering slopes and goats scattered as the car passed, tyres sobbing through the turns.

"Take it easy," Clay had muttered, half asleep as she left him. "There's no safety-net out there."

The village was piled around a small fishing harbour. A week ago, when Tony first appeared with her raffia basket and walked barefooted in trousers and bikini-top, the locals had no idea that anyone so desirably symmetrical could bring such drama and passion to the purchase of a few daily commodities. But word had since spread, and now she was greeted with respect as well as wonder.

Once or twice a week a coachload of crab-red tourists arrived and sampled the sucking pig at the restaurant on the quayside and ate the unleavened bread and went away; but today the village was spared. Tony finished her shopping and turned along the waterfront. Strangers nodded as she passed and she acknowledged each in turn. When she reached the restaurant she unslung the basket from her shoulder and seated herself at one of the tables on the paved area outside.

"*Un cappuccino*."

She lit a cigarette and glanced at *La Stampa*. Only a handful of people were there—a blue-chinned priest intent on his office, a couple of middle-aged women, heads close together, a powerful-looking man with the *Herald-Tribune* and a lip-line moustache who couldn't keep his eyes away from her. The coffee came and she added sugar. The world's news was as depressing as ever and she didn't dwell on it. She smoked the cigarette through, crumbled a biscuit for the pigeons, smiled to herself at the memory of Clay's involuntary fandango, paid the bill and left, retracing her steps to where she had parked the car.

Less than an hour after setting out she swung into the villa's short steep driveway. It had just gone five o'clock and the brassy glare had left the sky. She hauled her basket off the seat and made for the front door.

"Hold it!"

Startled, she turned. It was the man from the restaurant. As fast as light she wondered how on earth he could have got there so soon. And in the self-same instant she saw he had a pistol.

He was wearing a crumpled light-weight suit and carried an airline travel bag. With heightened awareness she noted his coarse brown thinning hair and the blue and white sweatshirt under his jacket.

He jerked the gun. "Take me through."

She wheeled around and did exactly as he said, opening the iron-studded door and leading him into the apparent darkness of the house. There was a yawning sensation in the pit of her stomach and, as they emerged on to the terrace beside the pool, the villa had never seemed so isolated. Clay was dozing, shaded by an umbrella, oblivious of his vulnerability.

"Who else is here?" the man said, right on her heels.

"Nobody."

"No maid?"

"No."

"Gardener? . . . Dog?"

"No."

The questions were over-loud, and Clay stirred. He opened his eyes and gazed at them both with bleary affability.

149

"Hallo," he said. "You caught me napping." Then he saw the gun and his expression changed. He sat up as if he'd been stung. "What the hell—?"

"Stay where you are."

"Who are you?" Clay squeezed his eyes against the light, bewildered now. Things like this happened to other people. "What's going on, for Christ's sake?"

"He was outside," Tony faltered. "He was waited for me."

"Go and join him," the man said. He used his head like a boxer. "Get yourself over there and speak when you're spoken to."

He was on the tall side, broad with it, all muscle. His accent was hard yet back in the throat. Whatever he was it probably wasn't American and certainly wasn't English.

To Tony he said: "Why's flatfoot got the bandage?"

"He twist his ankle."

"Oh yes?" The gun gave him complete authority. He came round the end of the pool. "Fine time for it to happen."

"Listen—" Clay began.

"You've got it inside out. My listening days are dead and gone."

"What the bloody hell d'you want?"

"We're coming to that," the man said. He sat on the edge of the second lounger, very sure of himself, looking them over. He put the travel bag down between his feet and took off his jacket, transferring the gun from hand to hand. His sinewy forearms were mahogany-brown; on one was tattooed MORGEN and on the other GESTERN. "We're going to do each other a good turn, you and the girl and me."

"We don't need any good turns."

"The fact remains that when I say jump you're going to jump. When I say move you're going to move . . . Like now, for instance. By way of example." He stood up and nodded at Tony. "It's time you showed me around."

She frowned.

"I want to see the house. And while we're inside," he warned Clay, "don't try anything foolish. Otherwise it'll be

150

the worse for her, and I've no wish for that. My part of this deal's to cause you no harm."

Tony led him into the villa. He was as quiet as a cat behind her. In the living-room she checked between strides for her vision to adjust and felt the gun touch her spine.

"Where's the telephone?"

She took him to the main bedroom. She pushed the door open and stood aside, but he signalled her to go on through. "What is the idea?" she began, white showing in her eyes, but the moment passed. He rounded the bed and ripped the telephone from the wall, a kind of savagery in the way it was done, as if to frighten from her mind any lingering suspicion that none of this was really happening.

He made a swift tour of the other rooms, not a word spoken, never more than a yard or two between them. In the kitchen he took a beer from the ice box and drank it from the can; in the garage he showed passing interest in the rubber suits and aqualungs. Otherwise he didn't pause. Within minutes he was prodding her out on to the terrace again and Clay was staring at them both with sullen impotence.

"There's a sensible guy," the man said. "Congratulations." The sun jazzed on the surface of the pool. "Ever seen a marionette show?" He produced what amounted to a grin. "The crudest pressures are the best—wouldn't you say that?"

"You're a bastard."

There was no reaction. He went where he had left the travel bag and tore the zip across. He reached inside and took out a walkie-talkie radio; it was black with white metal trim and had a shoulder strap fitment.

He said to Tony. "What d'you make of it?"

"I don't make."

"Specially designed for those who are out of sight but not out of mind."

"I don't understand."

"You will." He took a second handset from the bag and pressed a red button; three feet of telescopic aerial extended with a series of soft clicks. "Know how these things function?"

151

Tony shook her head.

"Come and learn."

She met his gaze. "And if I say no?"

"You don't look that stupid."

"I am not stupid enough to have printings on my arms either." Her anger flared, out of control. "*Morgen* and *gestern*—tomorrow and yesterday . . . What is it supposed to mean? Only peoples who have never grown up have words and pictures on their skin."

The man let fly, the point of his shoe making contact with Clay's injured ankle. Clay yelped and twisted away, his mouth an O.

"See what trouble you can cause?" the man said reprovingly. "Your friend could have done without that." His tone changed. "Get hold of that second hand-set and listen to me."

Reluctantly she picked it up. He began to explain how to operate it; nothing could have been more simple and she had no questions. The gun was always in evidence, utterly persuasive. Once or twice she glanced at Clay, conveying alarm as well as defeat. The man told her to go to the far end of the terrace and make contact, *sotto voce*, from there. After several false starts and shouted instructions to push the SPEAK or LISTEN switch their exchanges became reasonably proficient. Tony finally came through with: "Whatever you want we are not your kind of peoples. You made a mistake picking this house . . . Over."

"I never said to push your luck . . . Over."

"You are a bad dream." She was as petulant as a child. "Over."

"I'm flesh-and-blood real, and you know it . . . Over and out."

"For Christ's sake," Clay tried again. "Who the hell are you? Half an hour ago—"

"Half an hour ago, flatfoot, you were a non-contributing member of society. Once upon a girl's good time, and so say all of us, but there's more to life than lotus-eating. Very soon now you're going to make yourself useful."

Tony walked towards them. "You are all hot air." She was never able to hold her tongue. "All talk, all the time talk."

"Is that how it seems?"

"I think you are one big bluff."

The man fired into the space between Clay and herself. The gun spat and jumped in his hand and a beachball exploded behind them—all in an echo-less split second, so fast they hardly flinched. A fraction afterwards they blinked, caught their breath, stiffened; and a moment later the shrivelled casing of the ball slapped into the pool.

"God Almighty," Clay whispered. In terms of the bullet's path about two feet separated him from Tony; no more. The back of his neck prickled, ice and fire.

"Don't put faith in the bluff idea," the man said. "You'll only regret it . . . Let's have that understood once and for all. There's just the three of us and we might as well be together in a locked room."

A bougainvillaea-covered balustrade enclosed the near end of the pool. He crossed over to it, cryptic and shatteringly offhand, and looked out at the savage beauty of the scene beyond. Once upon a time the face of an entire mountainside had crumbled into the sea. Fantastic heaps of weathered rock now shaped the coastline, and the sea itself lay green and azure and gentian in a score of bays. The village was fudge-coloured in the near distance, and here and there were scattered a few medium-size villas, perched dramatically between sea and mountain, their stark newness redeemed by tamarisks and myrtle and splashes of flowers.

"Come and join me," the man said. "You, too, flatfoot. And bring the bag."

With difficulty Clay hopped across, unable to equate the man's conversational style with his reckless use of the gun, imprisoned momentarily in disbelief about himself and Tony and their situation.

"You'll find binoculars in the bag," he was told. "And a tripod. Let's have them out."

153

He had no choice. Despite their size the binoculars were surprisingly light.

"Try them."

He sighted on the villa known as Castello di Roccia. In all respects it was a place apart, incomparable in size and setting, rising sheer from the very tip of a narrow finger of land which separated one bay from another. Its stucco was the palest of blues, its huge area of ribbed roof a reddish brown. Terraced gardens faced inland and a raised driveway led to wrought-iron gates set in high colour-washed walls. Clay fiddled the soft blur into focus and the detail leapt at him across a quarter of a mile, fantastically sharp and clear.

"Good, eh?"

Against his will Clay nodded.

"Steady it on the tripod and you'll find it's almost too good to be true."

Sunlight lay across the sea like a bar of molten metal and the sea itself was a travel-brochure blue. The boat Clay used for water-skiing was moored in the horse-shoe bay below.

"Listen," the man said as lightly as if they were playing a game. "Who's heard of the Rivers diamond?"

Clay and Tony exchanged glances, but neither answered.

"Don't you read the magazines?" He was close, standing back a little, but the gun made him safe. "No? . . . Your education's incomplete. For your information the Rivers diamond is one of the big ones."

"So what?" Clay frowned.

"The Rivers diamond," the man said evenly, "belongs to a certain Barbara Ashley. And the Barbara Ashley in question—"

"God," Clay exclaimed, anticipating.

"—lives in the Castello di Roccia. And the Castello di Roccia, as you very well know, is straight in front of you."

Something seemed to heave in Tony's brain. She looked first at the man, then at Clay, then back to the man, transferring the same startled glance.

"Why are you tell us this?"

154

"Because," the man said, "I want the Rivers diamond for myself . . . And you're the one who's going to get it for me."

Time seemed to miss a beat.
"*Me?*"
"Correct."
"You're crazy." Tony tossed her head, incredulity in her voice. "I never hear such nonsense talk."
"You're getting it, beautiful, and that's that."
"How?" She fluttered her hands. "How? . . . It isn't possible. Besides—"
"It's possible, all right."
"Not by me."
"You better than anyone."
Clay said: "You must be out of your mind. She isn't a thief."
"There's always a first time . . . Give her the glasses," the man said curtly, "and let her see where she's going."
"You can't make her."
"You know damn well I can, so shut up . . . Now," he said with a nod at Tony, "take a long look—and listen like you've never listened before."
She lifted the binoculars to her eyes. He gave her almost half a minute to herself before speaking again.
"There's only one normal way in—along the driveway and through the gates. But that's hardly for you; Barbara Ashley doesn't exactly keep open house. And if you go over the wall you'll find the garden's alive with guards. What's more you'll still be outside the house. So you won't do anything like that."
She glanced sideways at Clay, appalled, tongue-tied.
"Keep looking," the man went on. "Look left, all the way left as far as the cliff edge. See the wall there?—like an extension of the cliff itself?" He waited, restless as a guide. "Right across from that cliff-edge part of the wall are two balconied windows on the second floor of the house . . . Got them?—between the casuarinas."
He took her silence for assent.

155

"The windows are the Ashley woman's dressing-room and bathroom—from left to right respectively. Nothing else need interest you."

To Tony it seemed they were almost close enough to reach out and touch. Yet in reality they were an almost impossible goal. In a voice that didn't sound much like her own she heard herself say: "This must be all a joke . . . Some kind of a joke."

"Ten seconds inside that dressing-room—that's all you'll need."

"I could never get there."

"A little help from me and flatfoot, and you'll surprise yourself."

"Never," she said. "Never."

"Tonight," the man continued relentlessly, "it's party time somewhere over Calagonone way—and the invitations include you-know-who. No ordinary party, believe me. The strongroom at the bank's already been visited with the occasion in mind. Which means that until the gates open and the white Mercedes drives her away the stuff I've set my sights on is in the villa for the taking."

"Tonight?"—this was Clay.

"Tonight, yes."

"Where did you hear all this?" Disbelief still sharpened his tone. "How in the hell—?"

"I've got friends."

"Not here you haven't."

"Here," the man said, "I've got accomplices."

Tony wheeled on him. "Why me?" She gestured almost pleadingly. "Why us?"

"Listen," he said. "When it's time we'll take the boat across to the base of the cliff. The two of us, yes . . . We climb the cliff together, descend together, return together. The only time you'll travel alone is from the top of the wall to the dressing-room and back again—and even then you'll have flatfoot whispering in your ear."

Clay scowled. "I don't get you."

"You'll guide her in by walkie-talkie. And the instructions

156

you give will depend on what you see through the Zeiss. The requirement is an empty dressing-room and with lighted windows and those binoculars you'll as good as have your own key-hole."

"Suppose the curtains are drawn?"

"They never are. She leaves the windows open, too."

"How d'you know?"

Again the man said: "Friends." He lifted his shoulders. "Observation . . . What are friends for?" He seemed grimly amused. "Barbara Ashley moves from dressing-room to bathroom, then back to the dressing-room again. Habit points to the dressing-room being unoccupied for fifteen to twenty minutes. That's when you two come into your own. The rest will be roses."

Tony had lowered the binoculars. She was pale and strained. "Those guards you talk about . . ."

"We've cheated them already."

"There is garden between the wall and that part of the house, the same as other places."

"Take another look," the man ordered. Then: "What else d'you see?"

"Where?"

"From high wall to window."

"Telephone wires?"

"Right first time . . . Just waiting for you to give a command performance."

Her eyes as she turned were wide with amazement, but for seconds on end it was as if she had lost her voice. "Do you mean . . .?" She faltered, got no further and tried again. "Do you seriously mean . . .?"

The man filled the hanging silence. "Why else d'you think I'm here, beautiful? They may not know it down in the village, but you're a very clever girl."

"Those wires would never hold me."

"Want to bet on it?"

"You bastard," Clay said with useless venom.

The gun made it all inevitable. The man's changes of mood were unpredictable, but there were going to be no deviations from his plan; that was a certainty.

"I singled you out," he told them, "and I've chosen my time. Don't kid yourselves along with fancy ideas that I might decide to cut and run. This operation's going ahead just the way you've been told."

Tony had no illusions left: the incredible was happening and she was a part of it. They watched the day die behind the purple mountainside. Bats began to flit and darkness spread like a stain across the water. The lamps of the distant village trembled brightly under the early stars. The Castello di Roccia seemed suspended between sea and sky, its shadowy bulk pierced by a dozen lighted windows. Clay had the binoculars trained on the only two that mattered; lit up and enlarged they offered astonishing detail. "Like I told you," the man said. "You'll be a regular Peeping Tom, so take care your attention doesn't wander." He made them practise with the walkie-talkie, sending Tony out into the night, extending the range. "Stay out of touch for more than thirty seconds and flatfoot's going to wish he never set eyes on you."

She kept slavishly in touch, and she came back. "Like a lamb," the man said, arrogantly confident. He showed no sign of nerves, but Tony suffered—chain-smoking, unable to remain still. At eight fifteen he got her to rope Clay to a chair set behind the tripod-mounted binoculars, and at half past he followed Tony down the rocky slope to where the boat was. They were wearing the rubber suits from the garage and were soon invisible. His parting words to Clay were: "Don't go silent on us, flatfoot. Don't ever let me get the idea you're trying to be smart."

He had no trouble with the outboard; one swing and it fired. He nosed out into the bay, throttled back and running quiet, handling the boat with a sure touch. Once they reached the open water he cut the engine and fitted the oars and made Tony row.

Quite soon he said to Tony: "Ask flatfoot if he can see us."

She called Clay, her voice low and surly. She had the walkie-talkie slung like a bandolier.

"Yes and no," Clay reported. "Only because there's a reason to look."

"Can you hear us?"

"No."

The sea was dead calm. Tony rowed them steadily past their own blunt headland and started in a wide arc across the next bay, traces of phosphorescence in the water, the cliff they would scale already looming, the villa on its summit already blocking out the lowermost stars. At most it took about fifteen minutes to reach the base of the cliff, during which Clay must have reported all of a dozen times. "Dressing-room and bathroom empty . . . No one there yet . . . Still empty, still no one there . . ." Only once was his whisper distorted, sucked away; otherwise he might have been with them.

The man steered the boat with uncanny precision, never hesitating, reading the darkness with impressive assurance. How he did it Tony neither knew nor cared; to the exclusion of everything else her thoughts were congealed around what awaited her at the top of the cliff.

"Both rooms still empty . . ."

Presently there was a soft grating sound. All at once the darkness was solid to the touch and they could smell the weed growths. The man grunted and ordered Tony to ship the oars. He worked the boat along with his hands. After about twenty yards they slid into a resonant gap beneath a flying buttress of rock where the water was as still as a pool. He made fast there, fore and aft, then clambered on to a ledge, hauling Tony after him. She could hardly see an inch and accepted his help, unconscious of the irony. Together they moved crabwise along the shelf until they were out from under the buttress and on the cliff face itself.

"Straight up."

She hesitated.

"You first." Even now he couldn't resist a jibe. "What kind of fool d'you take me for?"

She began to climb. To her relief it was easier, less sheer, than she'd imagined. She had no fear of heights and there were holds everywhere, hand and foot. Almost the worst thing on the way were the reports from Clay which prodded her mind where it least wanted to go.

"No one in either room . . ."

She lost track of time. Once or twice something broke off and rattled down. She was breathing hard and so was the man. When she looked up the stars thudded in and out of focus with every beat of her heart. Eventually she reached the top and lay there panting. The villa's wall stood several yards from the edge like a massive cake decoration. She stared at it, thinking back, thinking forward, no prospect of refusal or defiance remaining in her. Somehow it had come to this.

"The crudest pressures are the best . . ." *Madre de Dios.* "Do what he wants," Clay had urged anxiously. "He's trigger-happy. Try it, for Pete's sake . . ." All right. *All right.*

Presently she climbed on to the man's shoulders and hauled herself up on the wall. It was incredibly quiet and she moved with immense caution. A narrow width of the shrub-filled garden lay between her and the house. The balconied windows she had last seen through the Zeiss were off to her right, ablaze with light and partly hidden by trees, and she edged along to bring herself nearer, on the look-out for the telephone wires.

Without warning someone cleared his throat and spat. She froze, scared out of her mind, the pulsing seconds stretched into great distortions of time. At last she spotted move-ment—a dark figure passing away from her, patrol-ling a path under the lee of the house. She waited, flattened on top of the wall, until the figure had gone from view, and an enormous effort was required to force herself on again.

It was only a short while before she saw the twin wires. They stretched from above the dressing-room balcony to a gibbet-type post planted just inside the wall; the gleam of glass insulators located them for her. She began to work her way closer, dry in the mouth, still unable to see into the windows because of the trees.

But suddenly a shadow blinked the light from inside. And, almost simultaneously, Clay was through on the walkie-talkie.

"She's in the room now."

Clay watched Barbara Ashley enter the dressing-room and start to disrobe. She was a well-built blonde in her late thirties with three husbands already dead and a millionaire fourth just divorced. In other circumstances it might have given him pleasure. Twice she flitted in and out of the bathroom. Once, half naked, she stood before an ornate mirror and held a heavy pendant to her neck.

"Still there."

He was terse and to the point. He had had no glimpse of Tony and, since she called him from the boat, there had been no word from her either. It was beginning to seem as if he was talking to himself. Fretting, he pressed the SPEAK switch yet again.

"Still there."

Barbara Ashley chose that precise moment to step out of her pants and saunter more positively into the adjoining bathroom. Clay waited, allowing her a chance to change her mind. If Tony made a false start across the wires it could be disastrous. He delayed for at least a couple of minutes before coming to a decision.

"All clear . . . You can go now."

Once more he had this feeling that nobody listened. He screwed his eyes to the binoculars. A long time seemed to pass without anything happening and the beginnings of alarm stirred in his guts. Then, dramatically, he saw Tony silhouetted in space as she approached the window on the wires, small and compact, arms outstretched like a Balinese dancer. An exclamation escaped him. He watched as if mesmerised. She progressed with unnerving slow-motion and he sweated for her, the tension agonising. In a circus they would have been straining to applaud.

Eventually she came close enough to the balcony to be able to lower herself on to it. For a short while before she reappeared in front of the window she was lost to him against the dark of the house. The urge was to contact her, encourage her, but he fought it down. She darted like a shadow along the balcony, stopped, hesitated, then opened the window. A moment later she was inside and he held his breath as she hurried across the room, sharing the knife-edge seconds with her.

"Not only the Rivers," the man had said. "The rest as well."

It astonished Clay how quickly she emerged. He supposed the jewellery was on the table from which Barbara Ashley had picked up the pendant; at any rate Tony didn't have to look far. She came out, busily stuffing something inside her rubber suit. It was child's play—except for the wires. Her return crossing started him sweating again. Half-way over she suddenly stopped in her tracks, her silhouette absolutely motionless, and he guessed a guard was near. He pressed against the ropes, imagination on the rampage. When she finally moved again he began to tremble with relief, and by the time he reckoned she was off the wires and over the wall and on the way down the cliff relief had changed to exultation.

He continued his watch on the window. Barbara Ashley took her time in the bathroom and the boat was almost back at its mooring before she came out and theatrically discovered her loss. In fact Clay heard the boat throbbing softly into the small bay below at the self-same moment as the distant dumb-show panic in the Castello di Roccia got under way.

He waited impatiently for Tony and the man to arrive from the horseshoe beach. It was almost over; the future was about to begin again. After a while an area of darkness seemed to shift and he made out Tony on the path. But nobody else. Only Tony, walking up the path alone.

"Where is he?"

Even then he expected the man to answer. He peered past her, braced for the bullying voice.

"Where is he?"

162

"He won't be coming."

She was through the gate on to the terrace. "Not coming? How d'you mean?" There and then it seemed about the most unbelievable thing he'd ever heard.

"*Why* isn't he coming?"

"Because I left him there," she said.

His mouth was hanging open as she flopped into the chair beside him.

"What d'you mean—'left him there'?"

"He is at the bottom of the cliff."

An awful thought struck him. "Alive?"

"Of course alive."

"God," he said.

His brain seemed to have gone numb. He shot a glance across the water. Someone at the Castello di Roccia had switched on the floodlighting.

"He has what he deserve," Tony was saying. "Give me some cognac, please."

"How can I?" She seemed to have forgotten that he was bound to the chair. "Tony—what happened? For Pete's sake what happened?"

"I stole a lot of things, that's what happen."

He shook his head frantically. "To him." He was repeating himself. "What happened to him?"

"I gave him a push . . . Right at the finish, when we are both in the boat and the boat is not tied up, I gave him a push and drove off."

"Oh my God," Clay said.

"He was swearing something awful."

Clay swallowed. "Get me out of all this." She started to loosen the ropes. "What about the stuff you took?"

"He's got it."

"Oh my God."

"Not again."

"Huh?"

"That's all you say—oh my God this, oh my God that." She

freed the last knot and flipped the rope aside. "Get me the cognac, Clay."

"But that man—"

"Excuse me, but I have been up a cliff and over some bad wires and into someone else's room and down a cliff—"

"And incriminated yourself . . . Me as well." He was on his feet. "Of all the damn stupid things to have done. Don't you see? We're in trouble unless he gets away—both of us."

"I was made to steal. He force me. And you were tied up."

"Try telling the police that."

"It's the truth."

"Not the kind of truth they'll believe."

Clay went quickly to the binoculars and trained them on the base of the cliff, but he might as well have been staring into a dark tunnel. He straightened, agitated, urgency in every move he made.

"I'll have to go get him."

"You'll *what*?"

"We're sunk if he's found."

"Sunk . . . What is sunk?"

"To hell with that now," he snapped. "I'm going. Keep a look-out for me."

He picked up the walkie-talkie he'd been using and started towards the gate. Tony made a final show of bewildered protest.

"You're crazy. The way he treated you and me."

"That's not the point."

"It is ridiculous to have all that again."

"He won't come back here."

"If he still has the gun you will have to take him where he wants."

"All he'll want will be to get away. I'll dump him somewhere along the coast."

"Why not let him swim?"

He wasn't listening any more. She got up and went to the balustrade and looked over, watching the night swallow him

164

up as he hurried away. Her eyes narrowed in the star-green darkness.

"What happen to your ankle?" She'd intended waiting until later, but she couldn't resist it. "All of a sudden you lost your limp."

She went into the house and poured herself a cognac and got out of the rubber suit. She hadn't the slightest doubt about what she was going to do. Less than five minutes later she was in the Fiat and on the road. Half-way to the village a couple of cars crammed with *carabinieri* screamed by in the other direction. Around the next bend she pulled on to the verge and switched the engine off.

"Clay?" she said softly into the walkie-talkie. "Clay?"

He was soon there. "Yes?"

"The police are on their way . . . Over."

"Right."

". . . You found your friend yet?"

He parried it well. "Friend?" She could hear the muffled engine beat.

"Partner, then."

"What are you driving at?"

"You know . . ."

". . . Sounds to me you're off your head."

"Not any longer . . . flatfoot." Her lips curled. "Are you still listen?" She kept the thing on SPEAK. "Tell your friend he made one big mistake. Those printings on his skin—*morgen* and *gestern*. I saw those once before. The face I'd forgot, but not the printings—or where I saw them . . . It was in Madrid. He was reading a poster of *L'Oiseau d'Or* and it was the same day you later came and said to me 'Hallo'. At first I did not think it was possible. I told myself that I was making a mistake. But on the way down the cliff he forgot his game for a moment and mentioned you as Clay—which he could not have known. And so all the questions I have been asking come up with the same answer . . . You have been using me, flatfoot man.

165

You and your friend use me. You did a great big thing of make-believe together."

She relented for a moment and let him speak. "Tony?" he started. "What's got into you, Tony?"

"Goodbye," she said. "In spite of everything I hope you escape the police. You know why? . . . You never intend it, but you have been so very good to me." She laughed. "Don't be angry with your clumsy friend . . . Over and out."

She was far away when morning came, in another country. When she first opened her eyes in the hotel bedroom she couldn't for several long moments remember where she was; but everything soon jigsawed together. She felt under the pillow and pulled out what was there, staring with childlike wonder at the glittering brilliance of the Rivers diamond and the assortment of jewellery she had stuffed inside her rubber suit such an unreal time ago.

She was late down to breakfast, buying a newspaper from the stand on the way. An item with a Sardinia date-line in the second column leaped at her off the front page.

VILLA THIEVES' HAUL

Early this evening thieves broke into the Castello di Roccia, the Sardinian home of Mrs. Barbara Ashley, and stole a number of items of jewellery from her bedroom at a time when Mrs. Ashley was taking a bath . . .

"Coffee?" a waiter interrupted.

. . . How the thieves entered the house is a mystery, since the grounds are extensively patrolled. However, despite the audacity of the theft, Mrs. Ashley is not greatly concerned . . .

"Coffee?"

166

. . . "It was all imitation," she stated. "No one in her right mind would leave the Rivers diamond just lying about. Or anything else of value for that matter. I have a special arrangement with the local bank whereby—irrespective of the hour—I am always able to call at the premises and visit the strongroom en route to wherever I happen to be going."

"Coffee?" the waiter tried again.

Tears were rolling down Tony's cheeks; he hadn't noticed until now.

"I am sorry," he apologised gravely. "Is there anything I can do?"

She shook her head. To his surprise he realised she was laughing. In all his experience he had never seen such laughter. Baffled, he glanced at the newspaper.

"What is so funny?"

"Life," he thought she said, but she was so convulsed by that time that it was impossible to be sure.

Ten Minutes on
a June Morning

WEEDS GREW BETWEEN the worn cobbles, and the wall which enclosed the courtyard was scabbed with lichen. Behind the post set in the ground against the wall the ochreous stone had been smashed raw, and about chest-high the post itself was freshly splintered. A few metres along the wall from the post a gibbet rose out of a low planked dais. The rope was in position, running through a pulley fixed above where a man would stand.

Manuel Suredez noticed these things.

With the heightened awareness of fear his eyes took in every detail, his ears every sound. The courtyard was narrow, like a sealed-up alley, and no windows overlooked it. Half a dozen soldiers were present. Their uniforms were shabby, and one of them wore a cap with a broken peak. The Lieutenant, a little apart from the others, was smoking a cigarette.

Holy Mary, Mother of God, pray for us sinners now and at the hour . . .

The morning sun had barely cleared the wall and the long

Note: *Ten Minutes on a June Morning* won first prize for Francis Clifford in the short-story competition of the Crime Writers' Association. It was written in 1963, just before President Kennedy was assassinated. The author felt that its subject made it unsuitable for publication at that time; but later, with a change of setting and characters, he adapted and developed the theme for his highly successful novel *The Naked Runner*.

169

shadows of the waiting soldiers lay crinkled across the cobbles. Suredez was wearing rope-soled sandals, but the drag and clatter of the boots of the two guards between whom he walked reverberated about the enclosure. There was no priest. The guards did not speak. They led him past the post towards the gibbet; it was of pine and Suredez, one-time carpenter, noticed this also as the guards turned him and started to fasten his hands behind his back. One of the guards whistled tunelessly between his teeth.

Suredez quailed. A withering contraction began to shrink his insides, as slow and inexorable as the passing seconds. The last things he saw before a strip of cloth was tied over his eyes were the hairs poking through the pock-marked chin of the guard who blinded him and the Lieutenant heeling out his cigarette against the cobbles.

Holy Mary, Mother of . . .

He heard the two guards shuffle away. Then someone stepped on the dais and flipped the rope roughly over his head, tightening the noose around his neck. Light splintered through the coarse mesh of the cloth. Straining his ears Suredez tried to stifle the hammer-like thud of his pulse, desperate to identify the last few sounds that would measure off his remaining moments.

Not far away someone coughed, spat. A slovenly scrape of boots on the dais. He heard the pulley squeak as the slack was taken up; felt the rope quiver.

"Ready?"

The echo of the Lieutenant's voice fluttered around the courtyard. Suredez stiffened, trying to lift himself on to his toes, finger-nails digging into his laced hands, mind whirling. There was no need to drown to remember . . . Now it would come.

Oh, Jesus . . .

Silence.

Look down in mercy. Forgive me. Forgive us our . . .

Then a sound, slow and deliberate. The sound of someone walking. Half right. Coming closer. Suredez held his breath.

His lips continued to move, but no words, no gabbled whisper escaped them. Now he was listening again, wits resurrecting, still capable of wondering, senses clinging to life.

The footsteps approached casually. Two or three metres away they stopped. Another silence, careful, thought-out. Finally the Lieutenant spoke.

"The Colonel has changed his mind, Suredez." His voice was low, mocking. "He wishes to talk with you instead."

And Manuel Suredez slumped unconscious on the rope.

The man who dreamed this dream stirs on the bed in a room overlooking the Calle Sotelo in the city of Villanueva. The courtyard where this thing happened to him is seven hundred and fifty miles from Villanueva, but when he sleeps and the nightmare possesses him—as it always does—time and distance are destroyed. He surfaces with a start, the light of day breaking hard against his eyes, and a shiver passes along the length of his body as he stares about him and comes slowly to terms with actuality.

The girl is already awake. She sighs and moves closer, soft thigh, soft shoulder, dark hair touching his cheek.

"You're sweating again, Manuel."

June 14. The date leaps at him across the width of the room. He has escaped the nightmare, but not its consequences. Today is a day of obligation, *the* day, and he thinks with dread of the rifle in its case under the bath and what he must do before the morning is out; why he must do it.

"It is because you dream? You always seem to wake this way."

Suredez licks his lips as if to rid himself of the taste of death, but he does not speak. The girl chuckles through a yawn.

"What did you do, Manuel? What bad thing have you done?"

The office was small, pressed down on them from a leprous ceiling. A fan with only one blade churned above the desk like a dog in pursuit of its own tail. They had given Suredez an

171

hour after pretending to hang him before bringing him in to face this Colonel with the narrow head and beady eyes. There were some papers on the desk, weighed down by a glass ashtray. The Colonel frequently fingered his pencil-line moustache, as if to check that it was still there.

"Why do you imagine that you continue to be alive?"

Suredez had no answer.

"Yesterday we executed sixteen of your friends. They were shot. Did you know?"

"I was told."

The Colonel said quietly: "You personally killed five of my men." He tapped the desk. "Answer me. Is that not a fact?"

"If you say so."

"Five of the People's Militia. And the story is that you killed them in extraordinary fashion. The Captain who took you prisoner says he has never seen such marksmanship."

Suredez waited.

"Where did you learn to handle a rifle? Who taught you?"

"No one taught me."

"Have you always been so efficient with a gun?"

Suredez shrugged again.

"Captain Lozano is not given to exaggeration. But I should like to witness your skill myself."

They went outside into a yard. Another officer was waiting, a Captain, though not the one to whom Suredez had surrendered at Dove Bay. He was cradling a carbine. At one end of the yard were two poles with a rope slung between. Dangling from the centre of the rope was a metal plate of the kind prisoners ate from. The Captain walked away from them and plucked the rope. The plate jigged and swung in unpredictable fashion.

As the Captain doubled back, the Colonel said to Suredez, "Take the carbine from him. It is loaded. Take it and fire at that plate. But do not permit yourself any wild ideas. I will have a pistol against your spine the moment he hands it to you."

172

Suredez took the carbine from the Captain, his peasant's mind baffled, unable to grasp that he was already trapped. He fired six times at the plate as it jerked and spun in the bright air, hitting it four times despite the lingering nausea and the carbine seeming over-heavy.

The Colonel nodded admiringly and motioned to Suredez to precede him into the office. Once there he lit a cigarette.

"You are every bit as good as Captain Lozano reported. In fact I would say you are exceptional. Not many could do as you have done, let alone an hour after having a rope around your neck." He blew a thin stream of smoke which flattened and spread as the desk deflected it. "How did it feel then?"

Suredez had nothing to say.

"Not pleasant, eh? Not willingly gone through again, eh?" He tapped the desk. "Answer me."

"No."

"I do not expect it will be necessary," the Colonel said. He smiled, showing stumpy yellow teeth. "You look mystified, Suredez."

"I am."

"No glimmer of what we have in mind?"

"No."

"Then I shall tell you." The Colonel inhaled a curdled mouthful of smoke. "We have a job for you. A unique job. In the first place it will mean your being set free."

Suredez frowned his disbelief.

"I assure you," the Colonel said, "that I am speaking the truth. By tomorrow you will be on your way, though not your own master. No one will watch over you, but you will do what we require as surely as if you were still on the rope."

"What job is this?"

"You will dispose of someone. Tomorrow morning you will be on your way to Villanueva."

Suredez leaned forward incredulously. "But that is—"

"Exactly."

The Colonel watched him, narrow head tilted, a smirk on his lips.

After a lengthy pause, he said. "I can read you like a book, Suredez. I can almost see your mind working. There are two frontiers between here and Villanueva and you are thinking: 'How will they control me at such a long range?' You have a mother and a father and a sister. They live in the village of Los Santos de Maimona. Already they are under surveillance. This evening they will be taken from that village. Tomorrow they will be brought here. And if you do not do what you are going to be released to do they will be led out here and hanged. One by one. That is why we gave you a taste of it—so that you would remember. It wasn't nice, eh, Suredez?"

In the room overlooking the Calle Sotelo the girl sighs when Suredez does not answer and flounces on to her back, reaching round to switch on the radio. Music crackles softly. The sun is pushing long level rays over the roof-tops of the city and a reflection shimmers on the ceiling.

"Four nights," she says peevishly. "Four nights, and you have become as moody as a husband."

Suredez closes his eyes, the trauma of that other morning merging into the tension of the present. There must be no mistakes; no suspicions aroused. Soon the girl will rise and light the gas under the saucepan; wash and dress. Soon they will eat the claw-shaped rolls and drink the sharp, black coffee. Within an hour she will leave for the shop on the Plaza de Colon where she works in the shoe department. Then the waiting will begin.

"I'm sorry."

Now it is she who does not reply.

With satisfaction the Colonel noted the effect of what he had told Suredez—the blaze of hatred in the dark, bloodshot eyes; the clenching of hands.

"You wouldn't wish them to suffer in such a fashion, would you?"

"They have done nothing . . . Nothing."

"We aren't concerned with them, Suredez." He flipped his fingers twice, arm crooked, "But you are, which is as it should be."

Suredez reviled him, veins branding his forehead.

The Colonel merely spread his hands.

"Listen, Suredez. Listen well." Now there was menace in the voice. "You are as good as dead already, so we needn't dwell on the obvious. But if you refuse to travel to Villanueva, you will have murdered your mother and your father and your sister. If you change your mind after leaving here and do not go through with the assignment, the result will be the same. And even if you do not change your mind but fail to achieve what you have been sent for, they are the ones who will become fertiliser. Is that understood? There are no two ways about it. You will go to Villanueva as planned, you will make the necessary arrangements and you will ensure that the job is successfully completed. It is as simple as that."

The Colonel turned his back and stared out of the window, fingering his thin moustache. The silence closed in on Suredez. He put his face into his hands. Anguished little cameos of his sister and parents rose up to fill him with dread and appalled grief. He wanted to abase himself, to fall on his knees and plead, to tell the Colonel they had never indulged in politics or violence, how they had been dismayed that he—son and brother—should have done so. But even as his thoughts reeled and blundered in desperation, he was without hope. Justice was a word, love was a word, mercy was a word.

He raised his eyes, staring at the Colonel through meshed fingers. Even hatred had been bludgeoned out of him.

"Now d'you understand, Suredez?"

He nodded.

"You have no choice, d'you see?"

In a dry whisper Suredez said: "What am I to do?"

"I have told you. You will go to Villanueva and kill a man."

"Who? How shall I know him?"

"You will know him." The Colonel returned to the desk and sat down, grinding his cigarette-butt in the ashtray.

175

"Your difficulty will be to get close enough. Have you ever been in the city?"

"No."

"That country?"

"No."

"In the morning you will be escorted over the frontier. At the town of Chitros, ten kilometres beyond the border, you will board the Central American express. By nightfall you will be in Villanueva. There will be no problems as regards entry into the state. Your papers will be in order and we will provide you with sufficient money so that you will be able to fend for yourself during the required time."

"Who is the man?"

The Colonel propped sharp elbows on the desk. "The man," he said, "is the personal envoy of the President of the United States."

Beyond the Patio de los Naranjas in this alien city the great green bells of the cathedral boom the hour. The sound throbs into the room through the guitar-twang of the radio.

"What time is it?"

"Eight," the girl Dominga says.

"You'll be late."

"I won't, you know."

A movement distracts him. A small bird alights on the window-ledge, a cricket in its beak. There is no end to death. Suredez watches it, thinking, thinking. He will use this ledge himself before long; squeeze the trigger-finger and kill. Somehow he has to shut his mind to the victim's identity and think in terms of one life against three.

"You want coffee?"

He grunts.

"How pleasant you have become," Dominga says tartly.

She gets up and goes through the curtains into the recess which contains the bath and the tiny cold-water sink and the butane gas-bottle. He hears her strike a match and the gas "plop" as the stove ignites.

176

Suredez stiffened against the back of the chair. "No!" he said. "No!"

"What difference does it make? A man is a man, no more and no less. As far as you are concerned his office is unimportant."

"But—"

"You have killed before."

"Strangers. In action." He stared at the Colonel, numbed in a new way, in awe. "Oh, Jesus Christ," he said. Then: "Why? Why him?"

"It is considered necessary."

"Did you never believe in the revolution?"

"I took part in it."

"Then went sour. Lost faith. Turned traitor."

"New filth was being substituted for the old." Oh Jesus, Suredez thought. What has happened to me? His lips trembled. "I will fail," he said. "You expect the impossible."

"Nothing is impossible. In forty-eight hours you will be in Villanueva. In exactly a week from now so will the President's envoy. We cannot do more than bring you as close together as that. You know what will happen if you refuse to go. You also know what will happen if you do not succeed. The same things will happen if you should ever breathe a word where you are from—and this even after you have succeeded."

"And if I succeed?"

"You will have shaped the way the world is marching."

"What of my parents? My sister?"

"They will be released."

"For how long?"

"For as long as you remain silent."

"On what charge will you arrest them this evening?"

"We do not require to make a charge."

It always worries him when Dominga is behind the curtain, close to where the gun is hidden. He listens to her run the tap and begin to wash herself. A bed-spring clicks as he shifts his weight. Almost simultaneously there is a thud at the door as the delivery-boy tosses the newspaper across the landing. Suredez starts, nerves already wire-taut. He rolls off the bed and goes to the door, collects the newspaper and gazes down at it.

The headline reads: WELCOME SEÑOR! But it is on the thick-set, middle-aged face below that his eyes rivet.

The final thing the Colonel said to him was, "Do not have any illusions about your importance to us. Think rather of your importance to three people who will have been brought here from Los Santos de Maimona. They're expendable. Remember that should the fresh air of freedom affect your judgment. A thousand like them are expendable if need be. You won't be the last of our puppets if you fail."

He was taken away after that and photographed. Later, in a room somewhere off a musty labyrinth of corridors, he was given a cheap suit, shoes, underwear, socks, two shirts, a tie and handkerchiefs. They also gave him a second-hand grip and one hundred and fifty pesos in used bills. Early in the afternoon he was presented with a well-thumbed passport in which he saw himself recorded as Manuel Rodriguez, carpenter, born in a place he did not know by the name of Quelta. With it was an exit-entry visa on which was a Villanueva date-stamp.

After three hours of drilling, Suredez was word perfect. Eventually, he was left alone. There was no window to his cell. A raw, electric bulb gave light and his shadow moved endlessly across the flashing walls as he paced the floor, pride gone, courage gone, his will already tied to the strings that would ensure servility. Whenever he dwelt on what he must do his mind was pole-axed with renewed dismay, and when he thought of why he would attempt it he was almost unable to unclench his hands and unlock his jaws.

Home was the place where they always took him in, where his mother fussed to prepare a meal and his father listened to

178

him but did not understand and his sister gazed in rapture at the advertisements in old magazines that sometimes found their way to the small, cactus-fenced house. And now, because of him, the hard self-sufficiency of their lives had been stricken with alarm. Already they were on their way to this place, bewildered and afraid.

And here they would be kept while he went about their salvation. There was no way off the high wire unless he walked its full length and made himself an instrument of vengeance out of love for them.

Food was brought to him in the cell, but he had no stomach for it. Nor could he sleep. He lay on the straw-filled palliasse that served as a bed and watched a moth beat at the light until it killed itself; listened to the silence and wished himself already dead. At two in the morning he was still awake. They came for him then—three men with quiet shoes and sallow, joyless faces. The grip was already packed. Suredez picked it up and followed them through devious passages until they reached a door which opened on to a street and the quivering diamonds of the night sky. A car was waiting. He sat in the back between two of the men while the third one drove.

Nobody spoke, though once he was offered a cigarette. After nearly an hour they all quit the car and moved in single file through sugar-cane; then climbed between the steep, scrub-strewn breasts of hills. For five or six kilometres they kept together, more cautious sometimes than at others. At last they halted and one of the men said to Suredez, "We will leave you now. Keep on, as near to straight as you can, until you come to the high-tension wires. Go left—left, understand?—and follow them. They will guide you into Chitros before sun-up."

He was there at a quarter to six, entering the town as a crab-red dawn began to swell behind his back. At seven-twenty he caught the diesel express which came snaking out of the folded mountains.

And so it was that at eight that evening he finally reached Villanueva and went in search of a rooming-house.

179

"Ayee," the girl Dominga sighs approvingly as she wriggles into her clothes. "I like his face. I consider he has a good strong face. *Muy simpatico.*" She has taken the newspaper from Suredez. Now it lies unfolded on the bed. "A pity his wife does not come. It would be something to see her, too."

There is no traffic in the Calle Sotelo, cordoned off since midnight. Already the more curious are beginning to gather. The national flag and the Stars and Stripes hang limply from a score of windows opposite. In two and a half hours the procession will pass—first the jingling cavalry escort, then the wedge of motorised outriders, then the big black Cadillac and the accompanying cars. For perhaps twenty seconds the Cadillac will be within infallible distance of this second-floor window.

Dominga slowly zips up her skirt. She has to be at the shop by eight-thirty, but she seems in no hurry, humming as she studies the paper.

"You'll be late," Suredez tells her again. "It'll take you more than ten minutes the way things are shaping down there."

"Who cares?"

He masks his anxiety with a shrug. "It's your job, not mine."

"I wouldn't see much from the shop, anyway," she says, and his heart misses a beat.

"What d'you mean?" He faces her. "What d'you mean by that?"

The morning after he arrived in the city Suredez left his chosen rooming-house and went in search of the Central Post Office. His instructions were that a letter would await him. He entered the cool, echoing vault of the main building, approached the counter and spoke to the clerk.

"What is the name?"

"Rodriguez," he lied. "Manuel Rodriguez."

"Can you identify yourself?"

180

He placed his passport on the counter. Presently the clerk returned holding a long manilla envelope.

"You will sign, please."

Suredez signed awkwardly, lead in his heart. The strings were attached to him as surely as the Colonel had promised they would be. He walked across the patterned floor-mosaic, stopping by a battery of telephone kiosks. Furtively, feeling himself watched, he slit the envelope and extracted its contents. A folded rectangle of paper dropped into his hand. Opening this he found a small key with a cardboard tag attached. On the tag was typed a post-box number—Apartado No. 53. There was no note, but an explanation was unnecessary; they had told him what he would find when he used the key.

The glare of the Plaza del Pilar greeted him. He made his way to a café and, early though it was, braced himself with a cognac. He had six days in which to devise a plan. "The tactical details are your concern," the Colonel had said. "You know your capabilities. Like God, we are giving you a certain amount of choice."

A poster in a travel-agent's window caught his eye. U.S. PRESIDENTIAL ENVOY IN VILLANUEVA, it read. ROUTE SEATS NOW AVAILABLE. He went in and spoke to a girl at the desk. Yes, there were still seats to be had. Momento, and she would show him the diagram. She was back quickly.

"Here," she said, pointing a scarlet finger-nail. "This is the route the procession will follow from the airport to the Palace of Victories. They range from twenty-five to one hundred pesos." Now, as if for the first time, she seemed aware of his peasant's face, the too-large suit, his awkward hands, the cotton tie. And the tone of her voice changed. Acidly, she said, "How many do you want?"

"*Gracias.*" He backed away. "I will think it over."

Once outside he took a horse-drawn barouche to the Gran Via. Along much of its length scores of men were languidly at work erecting the timbered stands. He walked from one end to the other. It was wide, too wide. So was the Plaza de Colon. The Plaza del Pilar was more compact, but the Avenida de Zamora was even more spacious than the Gran Via. Yet he wasn't entirely discouraged. The Plaza del Pilar was linked to the Avenida de Zamora by a comparatively narrow street, the Calle Sotelo. Tallish, slightly down-at-heel buildings solidly walled its sides. Offices, consulting-rooms, apartments, a consulate—he studied the nameplates; gazed up at the balconies and windows.

Here? Somewhere here?

An hour later he retraced his steps, oblivious of the burning heat. Later still he rode in a bus to the airport, then turned about and travelled into the city as far as the Palace of Victories. By early evening he had seen nothing more suitable than the Calle Sotelo.

By then he was parched and weary. He ate and found his way back to his room, where sleep was merciful for once in that it claimed him quickly and allowed him to forget what he had been about, and why. In the morning, though, reality was waiting for him. He went early to the Calle Sotelo and began enquiring whether there was accommodation to be rented. He tried door after door, climbed stairs, rang bells, knocked, spoke with janitors and receptionists and tenants. And always he drew a blank. No, they said. Not even for a day? For half a day, even? No . . . By nightfall he despaired.

"Your problem," the Colonel's words had been, "will be to get close enough."

Choosing a pavement table beneath some blurred pustules of neon he watched the passers-by, filled with a terrible envy for the normality of their lives, their safety, their freedom; jealous even of the beggar who whined from the gutter. He ordered a cognac and sipped it; glanced at the newspaper. A White House advance party had already flown in, and as he read the list of names and their individual functions and considered the deadly efficiency of their security, the certainty of failure intensified. What chance had he got? How could he hope to match their elaborate precautions with nothing more

182

than a gun and whatever crude cunning desperation might lend him?

"A match, *por favor*?"

It was a girl's voice. He looked up. Unknown to him she had seated herself at his table.

"A match?"

Suredez nodded and fumbled for his box. As the match flared he held it to her cigarette and she steadied it, fingers touching his. Then, as the smoke cleared, quietly but point-blank she asked, "Would you like to come with me?"

He shook his head.

"It isn't far."

"No."

"Across the street, that's all."

Something turned in his mind. "Where?"

"Just over there."

"In the Calle Sotelo?"

"Yes."

He swallowed, pulse quickening. "All right," he said.

As they crossed the street together she was talking to a man who felt no lust, only relief.

Now she frowns. "What do I mean by what?"

"Not being able to see anything from the shop."

A puzzled lift of the shoulders. "Exactly what I said."

"But the parade goes through the Plaza de Colon."

"So?"

"So you'll be right on the route."

"And here I'm not, I suppose?"

"Here?" Alarm clenches in his chest like a fist. "I don't understand you."

"You would if you hadn't drunk so much last night."

"You're talking in riddles."

"I told you when you arrived back."

"Told me what?"

She let it drop like a stone. "That I wasn't going to the shop today."

A kind of vertigo assails him, as if he is actually falling. "Not going?"

"No."

"But you must." He feels his face twitch. "You must."

Another shrug, this time dismissive. She turns a page of the newspaper and begins to hum again.

In a voice that doesn't sound like his own, Suredez begins: "For the love of God, Dominga—"

"Oh, cut it out, can't you?" she flares. "Don't go on about it. I couldn't go there even if I wanted to. They've closed the shop up for the day."

When he first entered that tawdry room and saw the window overlooking the Calle Sotelo he knew at once that he would never find a better place. During that first half hour, when for five pesos he did what was expected of him, the hard core of his mind remained fastened on the promise of another possibility. Afterwards, as they lay on the bed and the neon blinking from across the street tinted their bodies, she said with meaning, "Was it because you were lonely?"

"Perhaps."

"Manuel, isn't it?"

"That's right."

"Where are you from, Manuel?"

"Quelta."

She laughed softly. "Country boy."

"Not any more."

"How long have you been in Villanueva, then?"

"Since yesterday."

"Doing what?"

"Looking for work," he said.

"What's your trade?"

"Carpenter."

"Well, I wish you luck." She got up and began to dress. "I also work, you know. Does it surprise you? I'm in the shoe department of the big store on the Plaza de Colon, but—

184

ayee—the pay is criminal." She blew smoke, sighing. "Criminal," she repeated indignantly. Outside, the neon pulsed on and off, on and off. "Where will you go now?"

"I haven't thought."

"You're an odd one," she said. "You didn't really want to come with me, did you?"

"I'm glad I did." As lightly as he could, he went on: "And I wouldn't mind staying."

"Oh, sure."

"Why not? It's an idea, isn't it?" He watched her intently.

"It's an idea, all right. I give you that."

They were silent for a while, but he could tell that he had planted a seed. More than most she knew about loneliness and the hunger for companionship. And presently she said, "Were you serious?"

"Of course."

"For how long?"

"A week, say. Until I find a job."

"How much would it be worth to me? I need to make fifty. Fifty clear."

"I could manage that."

"In advance?"

He nodded.

She'd been fooled before. "Let me see."

He reached for his jacket and extracted the rubber-banded wad of notes. Loose change apart he had ninety-five pesos left.

"What d'you say?"

Her answer was to count fifty pesos from the wad. Chuckling, she held them up. "Bed and breakfast, eh. God above, you have made me almost respectable! . . . But you'll have to be quiet on the stairs all the same."

And so began the mornings when they woke together and she hurried to the shop; the evenings when she returned and he fed her with myths about his day-long search for work; the nights when she lay with him and offered more than a few minutes of bought kindness. On the first morning he trans-

185

ferred his grip from the rooming-house. On the second he went to the Central Post Office and collected the gun from Apartado No. 53. It was discreetly cased, but as he carried the case back to the Calle Sotelo he sweated, half-expecting to be stopped and asked to explain what it contained.

Several times thereafter he took it out from its hiding place under the bath and fitted the gun together; renewed acquaintance with its balance and characteristics. He looked for a way of retreat once the crucial moment had come and gone; timed himself along the corridor and down the stairs that led towards a maze of alleys at the back.

Only on the third evening did he have a passing moment of alarm. Quite casually Dominga mentioned that she understood there had been a security check on the house. Good muscular control had never been one of his assets, but Suredez believed that he had managed to keep his face blank.

"What for? When?"

"The other day. Because of the American, I suppose."

"What did they want?"

"You'd better ask the janitor, if it worries you. It's flattering, I think. Makes one feel important, somehow." Her lips curled. "All the more reason for you to be quiet on the stairs, *amigo*. The janitor fleeces me five pesos a week as it is."

The days moved him steadily towards the brink. For all the waiting Suredez wasted no time, repeatedly rehearsing himself, checking and re-checking the gun, watching the pace of the traffic in the Calle Sotelo and calculating distances, seconds. So long as he remained alone he was better able to numb his mind to the reality of what was to come, but when Dominga returned from the shop and their two worlds overlapped, the strain of deceiving her and of masking his tension somehow tightened the skin of dread in which he existed. Sometimes, as she recounted the trivia of her day or sympathised with him over his failure to find a job, scenes from the nightmare overlaid his natural vision and he felt himself begin to tremble as if a fever were about to take him. Once, in the night, he woke twisting on the bed, roused by his own

186

voice calling, *Madre! . . . Padre!* Dominga slept on, but Suredez remained awake until dawn, engulfed by the ever-fresh terror of the courtyard and the blindfold, knowing these awaited them if he failed.

"Merciful Christ," he whispered to the fading dark. "How can you permit this?"

"*Closed?*"

"Closed, yes. Closed. Shut. Locked . . . Does that satisfy you?"

"What are you doing today, then?"

"I'm not doing anything. I told you last night. Why should I do anything?" Furiously, she mops the stove. "Anyway, what's it to you?"

"But you want to watch the parade."

"And so I shall."

Hysteria beats through him. "Look," he blusters. "I'll see what the agency can do about tickets. There are still some to be had, and if I'm—"

"You'll *what?*"

"Get some tickets."

"Have you gone mad?" Her look is incredulous. "What do I want with tickets. What's wrong with where I am?"

"A stand would be better."

"At a hundred pesos a time? It should be!" Arms akimbo now, lips curling. "And what d'you propose using for money?"

"I'll manage the money."

"Not for me you won't." She flings up her hands. "Jesus, Mary and Joseph, what's this all about? I've got a free day. I've also got a view of the route—a good one, too. And you start going off your head about it, pretending you're a millionaire—you without a job and only a handful of pesos."

Appalled, Suredez seems unable to move. Demented thoughts spin his mind. This room is the lynch-pin, and he must have it to himself. *Must.* And soon. No one must stand in his way.

187

"Listen," Dominga says. "You can do what you like, but I'm staying here."

Something explodes in Suredez, releasing him from paralysis.

Suredez hit her, harder, and she screamed again. The sound sliced through his brain like a knife. He dragged her from the window and flung her on to the bed, but she didn't stop; and every scream from her gaping red mouth was destroying his family seven hundred and fifty miles away. In panic he knew it, and in panic he could not quieten her. Vaguely he heard the stir in the Calle Sotelo; feet thudding on the stairs.

"Open up!"

He thought of the gun under the bath and started frantically towards where it was, at bay, reason gone. But the door burst open and two armed policemen shouldered in. He fought them off with a chair, but it was only a matter of time before they had him on the floor. They pulled him to his feet, right hand levered behind his shoulder-blades. Dominga lay sobbing on the bed, nursing her face.

"Murderer!" he bawled at her. "*Murderer!*"

The two policemen pushed him on to the landing. He continued to struggle. On the stairs, in the lobby, through the lane of sightseers he fought and shouted. The people stared and thought him drunk; shrugged their shoulders. Women. The trouble was always with women . . . A wagon drew up and Suredez was pitched into the back. And the sound of his agony could still be heard as the wagon accelerated away under the streamers hung to welcome the approaching cavalcade.